Satin Scars

Allison Santiago

Edited by: Heather Sims

Cover art by: Rebecca Richardson

Acknowledgments

To my dearest husband, David. Thank you for pushing me towards any goal. You have always encouraged me to pursue any venture I decided to take on in every aspect of life. You have helped me grow so much throughout the years without ever causing me to doubt myself. I love you.

To my children, Leyla, Elena, and Luca. You will always be my greatest successes. Because of you, I strive every day to be a better person.

To my sister and personal editor, Heather. You may not be my sister by birth, but you will always be my little sister. You have incredible talent and should never stifle your passions. You have always held my chin up when I was my own worst critic. Thank you for always supporting me.

To my "literary hype team"; Rachel, Patricia, Shelby, Bee, and Roxanne. You guys are truly amazing. Your excitement throughout my writing process is more than anyone could ever ask for and it kept me inspired.

To my dearest friend, Omar. Since the 8th grade you have been my closest friend and my rock through everything. You never allowed me to give up on myself and always encouraged me to be better. You were there during my darkest days and I will forever be grateful.

To Rebecca Richardson for coming up with an amazing piece of art for the cover. You took something and helped me bring it to life. Thank you.

To those who told me I'd never amount to anything or be capable of great things. Suck it. Your negativity gave me the motivation to prove you wrong.

∞One∞

"Well, here goes nothing." I said out loud to myself as I approached the doors of a great edifice.

Inside, my father, billionaire Thomas Clark, eagerly awaited my arrival. Growing up I never knew my father and he did not even know I existed. Not until I was eighteen and had escaped the clutches of UMBRA scientists, their experiments, and one extremely manipulative ex-boyfriend. The United Military Brotherhood of Righteous Ascension's mission was to start the next step of evolution and turn man into weapons. Which led my mother to give me over to UMBRA for their Evolution Project. Her hatred for my father led her to believe I could be used against him. After spending ten years locked away and tortured, I escaped my prison and found my father. Two years later, he finally convinced me to join him and others set out to end UMBRA once and for all.

Meanwhile in the conference room of the compound: Thomas Clark called for a meeting. He was a solidly built man, with dark eyes. His black hair and closely trimmed facial hair had subtle whisps of grey. Slowly but surely, Christian Wolfe, Tanner Morgan, Nadia Garin, Reed Forester, and Clayton Daniels all gathered in the room with Thomas.

"Okay guys, there is something I've been meaning to tell you. Almost two years ago, I found

1

out that I have a daughter. Yeah yeah, I know, shocking right?"

"Hold on, a daughter?! You found out two years ago and you're just telling us now?" Clayton, all but blurted from across the room.

Christian, snickered from where he was leant against the doorframe.

"Uhhhhhh, yeah, it was need to know and you didn't really need to know. Moving on." With a dismissive wave of his hand he continued, "She's on her way in to come stay with us here at the compound."

"So...how old is she and when does she get here?" a curious and excited, Tanner, inquired.

Thomas looked at his watch, "Don't even think about it, kid. And now."

They all clamored to get to the door for the first glimpse of the prodigal daughter.

I stood waiting as the team came hurriedly down the corridor in what I'm sure was meant to be a very inconspicuous fashion. I saw my father with his arms stretched wide.

"Kiddo!" The beaming smile on his face spoke of his happiness.

I wrapped my arms around him. "Hey dad." I couldn't help but to think to myself, "So this this is what a dad's hug is supposed to feel like." He then turned me to face the group.

2

"Guys, this is Karah. Karah this is most of the gang, everyone else is out doing god only knows what."

The first to approach me was a skinny kid, who looked to be a couple years younger than me. His baby like face and dirty blonde hair gave him a certain boyish charm. Then again that could also have had something to do with the Spiderman t-shirt he was wearing.

"Hi! I'm Tanner, Tanner Morgan. Can I get your bags and stuff for you?"

"Uhm, nah, it's fine, I got it. Thank you though."

Next thing I know a platinum blonde haired woman who has a serious case of "resting bitch face" approached me.

"Hi Karah, I'm Nadia, everyone here calls me Nova."

I could tell from the apprehension in her gaze that Nova didn't trust me. Her green eyes seemed to have thousands of questions behind them.
"Nova...that's a pretty cool name." I tried to ease her very obvious tensions.

"Give the girl some room or at least let her get out of the doorway." I heard a familiar voice, and a rush of reassurance went through me.

"Christian!!" I ran in to give him a big hug. I had met Christian on my last visit, where we ended up growing close. He was like the big brother I had

3

always wanted. He wrapped his arms around me and swung me in a circle, with a large smile spread wide across his face. Christian was the quintessential all-American guy with blonde hair, blue eyes, chiseled cheekbones, and a jawline that could cut diamonds. He was the kind of guy no one could hate, even if they wanted to.

"Come on, we got your room set up." Putting me down gently.

I walked down the hall with him and my dad. Christian opened the door to a room at the far end of the hall.

"This is your new room, if you ever need me, I'm right across the hall. Tanner is just down there, Nova is right next to me and Ryker, you haven't met him yet, is right next to you." He pointed to each room as he mentioned the corresponding name.

"Get settled and meet us in the common area. I want you to meet everyone else." My dad added, holding my shoulders, "I'm glad you finally decided to come home to stay." He kissed the top of my head and walked back down the hall.

"Home?" I thought to myself. Home was a concept unfamiliar to me, but I couldn't deny the happiness I felt.

I walked into the room and flung my bags on the bed and flopped backwards across it and sighed. The room was painted a light grey with satin chrome fixtures that matched the bedframe. A floor length mirror was attached to the bathroom door. I looked over at my reflection and saw only the girl I once was. My black hair was matted, skin paler than its usual shade of ghostly white. My eyes were gaunt and lifeless. I shook the image from my head as I got the sudden feeling I was being watched and sat up, propping myself up on my elbows. There was no one there when I looked up. The sun was starting to set on the compound and I then realized, I hadn't eaten in hours.

I spoke to myself, looking at my bags thrown haphazardly across the bed. "Fuck it, I'll unpack all this later." As I walked down the hall into the common area, I saw my dad and Nova standing around the island in the kitchen. On the unreasonably large horseshoe shaped couch I saw Tanner reading what I could only assume was a comic book and Christian smiled at me as I walked further into the room.

"Hey kiddo!" my dad greeted me with a smile. "Hungry?"

"Starving!"

"Pizza okay with you?"

"Dear sweet god, yes, that sounds perfect!" I enthusiastically replied.

With the mention of pizza, Tanner's head popped up. "Did someone say pizza?!"

I looked over at my dad, "He's an oblivious one, isn't he?" He smirked and nodded his head in agreement.

At that moment I heard a booming voice from behind me. "I have returned from my quest to retrieve the nourishment you mortals refer to as pizza!!" Without turning I already knew it was Atticus. Christian had told me all about the others before, but he was a memorable one. I turned around and came face to face with the navel of this mountain of a man, with long brown hair flowing past his shoulders. I could tell he was a very muscular man due to the proximity of my face to his abs. Looking up I saw a very large, accomplished smile on his face. Suddenly, his smile dropped.

"And who is this tiny being who is staring at me in a very strange way?"

Dad walked over as I slowly tried to back out of the chest of the delicious smelling giant...or perhaps it was the pizza, either way I realized I was too close for comfort.

"I almost forgot, not everyone was introduced yet. Atticus this is Karah, my daughter."

"Ah, welcome, tiny Clark!!" The joyful smile returned to his face.

"Did he just call me tiny Clark??" I said out loud, which caused scattered laughter within the room.

"Karah?!" A distantly familiar, high-pitched voice came from behind Atticus's massive body. I would know that voice anywhere.

"CHLOE?!?!?! Holy shit!" Chloe was petite with dark auburn hair and green eyes. Her bubbly personality always reminded me of Pinkie Pie from My Little Pony. She was the type of person who seldom got angry and always tried to see the best in situations. Which was the opposite of me and, honestly, shocked me considering how we met.

"Language!" I heard from Christian, who was now standing behind me. He always felt it inappropriate that I cursed as much as I did but, at this point, he knew fighting me on it was futile, not for his lack of trying.

"You two know each other?" Nova inquired with more suspicion in her voice than she meant to allow.

"Yeah, Chloe and I were in neighboring cells back when we were both hostages of UMBRA." A hush fell over the room.

"Did I forget to mention that this morning? Oh right, she was a hostage of UMBRA for ten years. They did their experiments, and she has powers because of them. Now," he clapped his hands together, "Who wants pizza?" That was my dad's best effort to change the subject.

"Dammit, Thomas." remarked a soft-spoken man who I already knew to be Reed. He was the closest thing to an uncle I had ever known. When he wasn't working in the state-of-the-art lab here at the compound, he was teaching at Columbia University. "Karah, mind if I draw some blood later?" his eyes shifted from my father to me, while looking up from the copy of *Journal of Molecular Science* he was reading. Reed, or as I called him, Uncle Reed, was a shorter man with light brown, curly hair that had developed a white patch at the front. His brown eyes were framed by thin wire wrapped glasses that tended to slide down his nose.

"That's fine, Uncle Reed. But can I eat first? I'm starving." At the mention of food, my stomach growled loudly. Desmond Bell and Clayton came in from the veranda that sat off the common room.

Desmond was a fit man in his late 20's, with a shaved head and cocoa skin. He had brown eyes and a goofy smile that could put anyone at ease. I could tell he had been a jock as a teenager simply by the way he had presented himself.

Clayton was a bit older than most of the group and wore a scowl much of the time. His left arm was adorned with a full sleeve of tattoos and his hair was buzzed in a military style cut. The emptiness behind his hazel eyes spoke of a rough past.

"Hey newbie, I'm Desmond, or Des, whichever is fine. And this grump here, is Clayton." Clayton glared at Desmond.

"Nice to meet you, Des. Hi, Clayton." I greeted them warily.

"Cara." Clayton reached his hand out for me to shake. "And it's Clay.".

"It's Karah, like Car-Ah." I shook his hand with a firm grip.

"I don't care." He walked away towards the aroma of the pizza.

As we all gathered on the couch to enjoy dinner together, Chloe and I caught up. It was then I had noticed, sometime during all the chatter, it started raining. Suddenly, the walls shook with a slam from the imposing front door. I whipped my head around to see who was coming in. As my eyes went across the room, I saw a man. A gorgeous, well-built, very drenched man. His dark brown, chin length hair was almost black as it fell in his face and dripped rainwater onto the floor. His crystal blue eyes that reflected the light from the lamps in the room were haunting yet captivating The water caused his soaked shirt to cling tightly to his body, allowing me to see the muscles underneath were well-defined and prominent. As my eyes panned down, even from where I was sitting, I saw the scars on his arms. My mind began to wander about things more salacious than the marks on his skin.

"Ryker meet Karah Clark, Thomas's daughter. She's going to be staying with us from now on.". The sound of Christian's voice snapped me back to reality and my face started to redden because I was caught staring. Ryker glanced away to my father, confused, and slightly annoyed.

"H-hi." I cleared my throat and tried to regain my composure as I stood to greet him, "Hi, I'm Karah." I extended my hand to him, which he responded to in kind as he placed his hand in mine. His handshake was firm but not aggressively so. It was also surprisingly warm despite the fact he was soaked to the bone.

"Hi Karah. Tristan Ryker. Nice to meet you." Giving me a forced half grin, he looked up to the rest of the room, "I'm going to go change into something a little less...wet." Even just hearing him say the word, *wet*, made my body tighten.

"Dear sweet mother of god, this man is something else." I thought to myself.

As he walked away, I could see him start to strip off the saturated shirt, which revealed his broad, muscular shoulders, defined back and more, much deeper, scars. His jeans rested on his hips and tightened around what, from all appearances, was an ass taut enough to bounce a quarter off. I leaned over to keep him in view, not realizing I had leant just a bit too far and went crashing into Tanner's lap.

"Holy crap! Are you okay? Did you pass out?! You locked your knees, didn't you? You should never lock your knees when you're standing." Tanner declared at an alarming speed as he fawned over me.

"Yeah...my knees...that's what happened. I'm fine." I stammered as I attempted to scramble off his lap. At that point I could do nothing but laugh at myself for acting like a giddy schoolgirl with her first crush. "Sorry about that Tanner, I hope I didn't hurt you."

I could see him blush but only just. "No, I'm good. You can fall on me any time." He told me with a smile before his eyes widened, "Oh, that came out wrong." He glanced at my dad. "Sorry Mr. Clark, that is NOT what I meant!" The entire room burst into laughter.

Uncle Reed stood up, "Hey, Karah, it's getting late, can I go ahead and get that bloodwork before you go to bed?"

"Oh, yup. Yeah. Lead the way, Uncle Reed." I brushed myself off. It didn't take long for Reed to draw the blood he needed. But by the time he was done, I could feel the day taking its toll on me. I went back to my room, where I realized I still hadn't unpacked.

"Fuck." I sighed.

"Language." I heard from the doorway behind me.

I jumped and whirled around, "Jesus Christ, Christian! Don't sneak up on me like that!" He laughed as he came into the room.

"You want some help?" He asked while he crossed his arms with a smile. A smile at my expense.

"Yeah, that'd be great." I nodded thankfully. I opened the drawers of the dresser and started to put my clothes away. Christian began to help, pulling clothes from the open bag on the bed. In doing so, he grabbed a pair of lacey black thongs.

"Oh!! No! Who exactly do you need THESE for?!" The look of horror that was on his face was priceless as I snatched the unmentionables away from him.

"No one in particular...yet." I told him with a cheeky grin.

"Mmhmm. Which reminds me, what was with the falling over earlier? Was that because of Ryker?" He asked with a knowing look in his eyes.

"What?! No! Of course not. No." I shook my head while I tried my best to sound convincing.

"Riiiiiiiiiight." Christian said with a smile. "Just be careful. Ryker may be my best friend, but he has his issues." The smiled dropped from his face as he looked into my eyes to convey his seriousness.

"Get out!" I laughed and started to push him to the door. He threw his hands up with a shake of his head as he walked out.

After Christian left, I finished unpacking my clothes and got into bed.

What felt like just minutes after I had fallen asleep, the sun peaked its golden rays through the curtains and across my face.

12

"Ugggggggh, curse you evil day star!" I groaned and attempted to cover my face with a pillow.

"Rise and shine sleepy head!" I heard Chloe's sing-song voice from the door, which caused me to promptly throw the pillow at her. Giggling, she came bounding onto the bed, her dark auburn hair glowing in the morning sun like a burning ember. "Wakey wakey!" She started poking me in the ribs.

"Chloe, sweet baby Jesus, whhhhhy?!" I whimpered, still half asleep, trying to swat her hand away from me.

"Because we have many things to do. Like training. And..." She leaned closer to my ear, "shopping!"

"Did you at least bring coffee?" I asked hopefully. "You better not have woken me up this early without the delicious anti-murder bean juice as a token of apology."

"Yes, but it's on the dresser, you have to get out of bed to get it." I could hear the laughter in her voice as she nudged me.

I moved the hair from my face and looked at Chloe with only one eye open. "I hate you. You know that right?"

She stretched out beside me, "No, you don't."

Another voice came from the doorway. "Snuggle party?! Count me in!"

In unison, Chloe, and I both yelled out, while letting out a childlike giggle, "GO AWAY, TANNER!"

I got up, got ready for the day, and walked into the common area with the coffee Chloe had brought me.

"Ready to start training, sweetheart?" Dad had just walked in from his office.

"I mean, I guess. Training for what?" I asked him skeptically.

Nova walked in from another room. "We need to first see what powers you have. After that we can decide what you need to work on, what you are already capable of doing, and where your physical abilities are at."

"Uhm, ok...but I'm going to need a volunteer."

Tanner couldn't help but to pipe in. He raised his hand as he said, "I'll do it! I mean...as long as I don't get hurt in the process." I could tell he was second guessing his hasty agreement as his arm started to lower.

"You won't. I won't do anything to hurt you." I tried to comfort him with a watery smile.

Nova, Tanner, my father, and I all made our way to the training room. My eyes widened as I saw how massive it was. On the far-left side of the room, a variety of workout equipment and free weights were available, all organized by the lightest to the heaviest. On the furthest right side of the room, a

14

row of heavy bags hung. Some were worn as others looked newly replaced, and I couldn't help but wonder how many were due to Ryker and the obvious strength he possessed. "Stop that," I chastised myself with a shake of my head. I was SO not here to fantasize about a man I barely knew. I walked to the center of the room after my slight lapse in concentration. I bounced on my toes a couple of times to loosen up.

"Ok, Stretch, you ready?"

"Coming! Where do you want me?" Tanner questioned with that boyish grin of his.

"Just stand anywhere...here-ish." I told him while motioning with my hand in front of me. Tanner walked over to the area I indicated, there was only a slight shake in his hands.

After a quick glance around the room, I closed my eyes, took a deep breath in, and concentrated. Remembering how I channeled my power before in order to escape UMBRA, I opened my eyes. Rather than their original amber color, they had changed to a brilliant violet hue. I raised my hand to my face and blew over the palm, the breath rushing across my hand released a violet cloud that enveloped Tanner.

"What does that do?" Nova seemed unimpressed.

"Well, what do you want him to do?" I asked off-handedly.

15

"Oh! Make him do the chicken dance!" Des shouted as he flapped his arms. At some point, Des, Christian, and Uncle Reed had joined us in the training room. I looked at Des and shrugged. All the while, Tanner stood completely motionless in the middle of the dust.

"The chicken dance it is." I thought of the ridiculous dance, the movements, and motions. Suddenly, Tanner began to do the absurd jig. Stunned silence was all there was throughout the room. I looked at every one in turn and then I thought for him to stop. His movements followed my thoughts, and he ceased his dance. I once again closed my eyes and breathed out. When I opened my eyes, their natural color had returned, and Tanner collapsed to the ground. Uncle Reed rushed to his side and knelt beside him.

"He'll be okay. He's just going to sleep for a few hours." I reassured everyone, although, I had only used my powers a handful of times. I was really trying to reassure myself.

"Interesting." It was the first time my father had spoken since we had entered the training room.

"That's kind of badass!" Des exclaimed. He was holding his hands above his head like he just scored a goal, and that only reaffirmed my suspicions of his jock background.

"You seem to have a pretty decent grasp of your power." Suddenly, Nova seemed a touch more impressed with what I could actually do.

"Except the fact that it doesn't always work when I want it to. Or as fast as I need it to. Trust me, if it had, I wouldn't have stayed with my ex for over a year." I crossed my arms over my stomach protectively, which I caught myself doing when I thought of that low point in my life.

"Well, let me run some tests on whatever that dust was that came from your hand, I'll see what I can find out about its properties." Uncle Reed carefully picked Tanner up off the ground. "Someone should probably put the kid to bed."

"I'll make a call to Marcus Miller. See if he can come in and help you learn how to get your powers to work when you need them to." My dad's arms were across his chest and a look of concentration on his face. He looked over to me and smiled, "Good job by the way." He mentioned before turning and walking out of the training room.

"Good job? Is he…proud?" The thought crept across my brain. Parental pride isn't something I was accustomed to, but I couldn't help the rectitude I felt with it.

Nova began to walk toward me with a smile. "Now it's time for the real training."

"Real training? Wha-!" I could feel my feet fling out from under me with a powerful kick from

17

Nova. Where she once stood, she was now crouched with one leg out straight from where she swept my feet out from under me. I gave her a smirk as I started to rise. "Ah, so that's how it's going to be." I got into position across from her and she did the same. We sparred for the next two hours, keeping toe to toe.

Her breathing was coming as hard as mine. "Not bad." She commented frigidly. I could see I was starting to break through her barrier.

"Thanks, Nova." I wiped the sweat from my face and ignored her tone, "I'm going to take a shower. Chloe wanted to go shopping." I started to turn and leave the room.

"Right. Well, have fun, I guess. Oh, and watch her at the Dippin' Dots stand, she loves those things." We parted ways, her walking towards my dad's office and me towards the common area.

As I walked past the couch towards my room, the only thing I could think of was my father telling me "good job". My mother was a bitter woman as far back as I could remember. To a certain extent I think she resented having me as her child, and she only kept me from my dad because she hated him more than she loved me. I was so lost in thought I didn't even realize that someone was in front of me until I slammed into them. It was like hitting a brick wall...with my face.

"Owe! Shit, sorry, I wasn't- "

"Paying attention?" Ryker finished my sentence before I could get it out of my mouth. "I noticed." His reply was dry and sounded as though he were annoyed at the fact I ran into him. "Are you okay?"

"Yeah, I'm fine." I looked up at him, my cheeks grew hot due to sheer embarrassment and the close proximity between our two bodies.

"Yeah, I don't think so. Your nose is bleeding." His tone was full of amusement as a slow smirk crossed his face.

"Dammit!" I immediately put my head back to not drip blood on the floor. I clenched my eyes shut, not from the pain, but from the downhill turn this encounter has taken.

He rolled his eyes. "It's okay, we'll get you fixed up. Come on." With his strong, scarred hand on my lower back, he led me to the kitchen. "Sit here." He guided me to a stool placed at the edge of the island and helped me sit. After he was sure I wouldn't fall, he stepped away from me. I could hear him rummaging around and the rattle of ice. He came over and gently moved my hands from my face and placed a bag of ice on my nose.

"Wouldn't want those pretty eyes of yours to be all black and blue." He smiled and his tone changed.

I give him a half grin. Blood pouring from my face is not a good look to try to flirt with, so instead of embarrassing myself further, I kept my mouth shut. After a few minutes, the bleeding stopped and I was able to drop my head back down, my eyes fell immediately to my lap.

"I think I'll be okay now. Thank you. For helping me." I hated the shyness in my voice. I was outgoing, considering my past. This man just did something to me that was unexplainable.

"My pleasure, doll." Was that a hint of softness in his voice I heard? No, it couldn't have been. There was nothing soft about the man standing in front of me.

"Doll?" I hate pet names like that. As if I were a fragile porcelain toy. I opened my mouth to object to the name as our eyes met. I lost myself in the clear blue waters of his irises as all thoughts escaped me. He brushed a hair from my face, his focus never left my eyes. The sensation of his hand against my skin sent a tingle through my entire body and I shivered. The twitch at the corner of his lips was the only indication that he knew what had just occurred.

"Karah?!" Chloe shouted from behind me. "Did you even hear me?" The moment was broken and we both blinked a few times as the rest of the room came back into focus. His hand dropped as he straightened and took a step away from me.

"Huh, what? Yeah...no." My brain was still trying to understand what had just happened. One second Ryker was a cold, uncaring bastard and then the next he's sweet, kind, and all around perfect. I couldn't decode him, and it was giving me a headache trying to figure out the puzzle that was Ryker.

"I asked if you were ready to go, but clearly you need a shower..." There was a teasing to her tone, "a cold one would be advised." She laughed. "Sorry Ryker, I have to take your captivated audience now." She said while pushing me out of the chair and edging me out of the kitchen towards my room.

"Don't. Not a word." I looked over at her with my finger pointed at her. She just chuckled and held her hands up in a conceding way.

After taking a shower and getting dressed, Chloe and I spent the next few hours shopping. I gave in and let her have a small cup of Dippin' Dots, but we didn't have to tell Nova that.

It was dusk when we arrived back at the compound carrying the spoils of our adventures. Including one skin-tight, thigh length red satin dress that I knew my father would never have approved of. But I figured I won't be young forever, so why the hell not.

As we entered, Atticus was in the kitchen wearing an apron that was far too small for his monstrous size that read "*Kiss the cook*" across it.

"Ah tiny Clark, you have returned! I will be trying my hand at cooking, anything you would have me create for you?" He had a spoon in one hand and a pair of tongs in the other. I raised an eyebrow at him and contemplated if we would have to call the fire department or not.

"Seriously, with the tiny Clark again?!" This man was exasperating.

"What? You are of Clark blood and you are tiny." He replied with an innocence in his voice and a smile in his eyes.

Glaring at him for a moment, I shrugged my shoulders, "Alright, I guess that's fair. But you're the only one who can call me that! And whatever you want to make is fine by me." I started to walk towards my room when I turned back to him, "Just don't burn down the compound." I added with a smile as I continued backwards.

He grinned his enthusiastic grin. "A feast it shall be!" He raised his arms, with the cooking implements still in hand, in victory.

I took my bags and put everything away in my room. After the literal feast Atticus prepared, it wasn't long before exhaustion set in and I made my way to bed. I once dreaded the times I had to lay down. Up until I was united with my father, sleep was hard to come by. The nightmares and visions of my past wouldn't allow for it. But now, falling asleep was almost instant.

∞Two∞

It had been six months since I had joined my father at the compound. I continued to train my physical abilities with Nova and began training my powers with Marcus Miller. Marcus was tall with dark salt and pepper hair, his dark eyes had wrinkles that began to form at the corners. His nose was crooked where it had obviously been broken. His hands were steady, and he was a master at meditation and inner spiritual mumbo jumbo that I probably should have paid attention to. Which I would have, had it not been for a shirtless Ryker training at the other end of the training room. I found myself looking his way more often than not, but I also saw him watching me from the corner of his eye when he didn't think anyone was looking. Marcus was one of UMBRA's first successful test subjects with the power to teleport. Him and his brother had been abducted as children and made to endure the same tortures that I had. His brother was a failed test subject, the torture and experimentation made him slowly lose his mind until he was nothing more than a withered shell. The brotherhood wouldn't tolerate failure. I had learned that everyone at the compound had a hatred for UMBRA for one reason or another.

As the days crept by, I learned more about my newly found family and how they came to be at the compound. Nova seemed to be trusting me more as the days went on. Clay was still very standoffish towards me. Although, I couldn't understand why. Chloe and I had once again become close, and she and Tanner had become extremely close. Christian was my best friend, my confidant, and my rock. When the nightmares returned, he was there to comfort me. Often times hugging me close and speaking words of reassurance late into the night. Atticus, I had come to learn was also an experiment success. Taken along with his brother and sister, who he had not been in contact with since their escape, 5 years ago. He had super-human strength that rivaled many fictional characters. His slightly terrifying ability to bench press a school bus was evened out by his mild temper and comedic ways.

And then there was Ryker.

Ryker still confused me on a multitude of levels. While his hot and cold act remained, the game of cat and mouse intensified. Sexual tension and flirtations that seemed to make a few of our housemates uncomfortable and possibly even a little jealous occurred regularly. However, I only knew of him what Christian would tell me. Like the fact that he wasn't taken by the brotherhood as a child, as most of us were. He was a soldier who went to war and after taking an IED to his hum-vee, had woken up at an UMBRA facility. The brotherhood's experiments turned him into a nearly indestructible super soldier who had extreme strength and arbitrary amounts of speed. He too had nightmares that woke him in the middle of the night. Like many of us, he was also a success and his hatred for the brotherhood was rivaled only by my own. I wanted to know him more. I needed to. Call me crazy, but I NEEDED to know what made him tick, what made him the way he was, and what caused the clenching in his jaw whenever the brotherhood was mentioned.

It was three days until my twenty-first birthday. I woke and began to start my day as I would any other. I donned my training clothes, a standard black sports bra, athletic pants tight enough not to hinder my movements and my tennis shoes. I threw my ebony hair in a sloppy bun and went out to join the others for breakfast. As I sat down to my healthy bowl of Lucky Charms, my dad slid into the chair next to me, put down a cup of coffee and smiled.

"Hey kiddo." He was still holding the clown like smile.

"Yeeeeeees?" I knew I sounded skeptical.

"What do you want to do for your birthday?" He leaned an elbow on the island and set his chin in his hand. His eyes never lost the smile, and he had a smirk pulling at the corner of his mouth. I could tell he was up to something and the only way I would get answers would be to play along.

I never really had celebrated my birthday before, so I never thought too much about it, or what people ever really did. "Oh, uhm, nothing, I guess. Wait, how did you know it was my birthday? I never told anyone that." I turned questioning eyes to my father.

"Nonsense!" He exclaimed with a perplexed look on his face. "This is what is going to happen." He sat up straight and clapped his hands together. "You, Chloe, and Nova are going to go shopping, get yourself something stunning. Formal. Yes, definitely formal." He nodded his head at his own reasoning. He sat forward and put his hand on my shoulder, "And do you honestly think it was hard for me to find out when your birthday is? Please, I did that the day we met." With a playful eye roll he sat back again.

I realized that made perfect sense. A nineteen-year-old showing up at his door saying they were his long-lost daughter, of course he would want to do some digging.

"Dad, really, you don't have to do anything." I could feel myself blush. For some reason I had suddenly felt a mix of shame and embarrassment. Not just that I expected my father to not know my birthday but the fact he wanted to celebrate it. No one had ever cared before.

He stood up and slid a black credit card over to me saying, "Here, you ladies go have fun. I'll make all the arrangements."

"Dad, I have training, I can't." I attempted to slide the card back to him.

His head snapped up and scanned the room, finding Nova, "Nova, no training today, you guys are going shopping." He glanced at me with a winning smile on his face.

To this Nova rolled her eyes, "I'll go change." She called out as she walked away.

I looked down at myself. "Yeah, since there seems to be no getting out of this, I should go change too."

My father had an all too pleased with himself look upon his face and winked at me. I walked away to find Chloe and let her know what the plan was for the day. On second thought, since she's telepathic, I figured that was pointless and redirected my path to get ready. As I walked down the corridor to my room, Ryker was in his, back to the open door. His shirt was, well honestly, I couldn't have cared less where his shirt was. He was wearing nothing but grey sweatpants that he filled out in all the right places. I couldn't help but stop and take a moment to appreciate my luck to be passing by at that exact moment. But up until that moment, I had never seen his scars that closely. Hundreds of them, all over his body. I could tell many of them were once deep wounds.

My gaze traveled up when he spoke, "You know there's a mirror here, right?" My gaze snapped to his in the reflection and as he turned to me. He asked, "See something you like, doll?" with his stupid, sexy grin and a playfulness in his eyes.

After my brain caught up with what was happening, I raked my eyes slowly down his body again, "Would it bother you if I say I did?"

"Nope." He stepped closer to me. His body looked as though he had just walked out of Olympus. A thin line of hair leading from his navel straight down into his sweatpants. The V-shaped lines were like glorious arrows pointing to the bulge in his pants as though it were a gift, waiting to be unwrapped. I was more than willing to be the one to pull that bow.

I swallowed. Hard. "Think of something clever to say dumbass!" Was apparently, the only thing I could think at that moment. I opened my mouth to speak, but no words would exit. He bit his lower lip as though he were waiting for me to make a move. He brushed the back of his hand against my cheek. Suddenly, I heard someone had cleared their throat behind me. I whirled around and could feel the heat in my cheeks.

"Uh Karah, GO GET DRESSED!" Squealed Chloe in a pitch much higher than her normal squeak. Which I had learned she did when she was excited.

Ryker smiled, leaned closer to me, and whispered, "Next time, doll." His voice had a seductive quality to it that made my insides clench and the blush creep up my neck. I heard his low chuckle as I'm sure he could see the effect he had on me since my hair was off my neck.

I glared at Chloe, as I walked past her, "One extra minute, you couldn't have given me one extra minute...asshole." While I hadn't actually been angry with her, the sexual frustration was getting the better of me.

"You need to get laid." She giggled as she wrapped her arm around my waist.

"Hate you!" I snapped, laughing, as I tossed my arm over her shoulders.

I had changed clothes, taken my hair down and Chloe, Nova and I were off to find something formal for my birthday party.

"Uhm, guys...where do we find formal gowns?" I had never been to any sort of celebration or formal event, so I was completely out of my element with this.

Nova looked over at me, "Don't worry, there's a place already waiting for us." She seemed so nonchalant and carefree as she looked at the scenery flowing past the windows of the car.

We arrived at the store and two men wearing suits opened the doors for us.

"Welcome ladies, we've been expecting you." One of the men greeted us. As we walked in, a woman who appeared to be in her 60's approached us. I could see that her once seemingly blonde hair was almost completely white and was pulled into a tight bun on the back of her head. Everything about this woman oozed poise and class.

"Welcome Karah, I am Mrs. Corbyn. I have been your father's personal stylist for over twenty years now. I have made some selections for you. They are hanging in that dressing room." She introduced herself with a nasal British accent and pointed a skeletal finger toward a door in the back of the shop. "Good to see you ladies again." She addressed Nova and Chloe with a nod of her head.

"Dad has a stylist?" I whispered to Chloe in awe. She nodded with another of her trademark giggles.

As I entered the dressing room, I was met with some of the most hideous articles of clothing I had ever seen. I riffled through the rack of dresses, tried some on, immediately hated them, and repeated, until I came across a stunning black dress. It was haltered and low cut in the front. The cut ended between my sternum and navel, accentuating my cleavage. The skirt of the dress was made of tulle and satin and cascaded to the floor with a slit up the left side to just below my hip. I looked at my reflection in the mirrors that were surrounding me. I slid my hand down the sides and made an amazing discovery that every woman loves.

"Wow…my tits look fabulous!" I grabbed my chest. To which I heard laughing from Nova and Chloe in the chairs outside the dressing room.

"Come on Karah, we want to see!" Chloe said with a hint of excitement and impatience in her voice.

I took a deep breath and emerged from the dressing room.

"Whoa." For a moment, Nova uncharacteristically dropped her bitch face.

"YOU LOOK HOT!" exclaimed Chloe as she bounced up and down in her seat.

"Thanks…it has pockets!" I shoved my hands in the pockets of the gown and flapped my hands as if they were wings.

After buying the dress we returned to the compound. A young woman I had never seen before and my father stood over folders strewn across the island. She was beautiful, with silky dark brown hair and caramel colored skin. She was wearing an elegant olive blouse and fashionable black business pants, paired with black stiletto pumps. I then understood why any man who entered the room stopped to stare.

"Who is THAT?" Even to me, my voice had a touch more annoyance in it than usual.

Tanner who happened to be the closest to us as we entered, answered my question with a dreamy sigh, "THAT is the party planner."

I saw a flicker of jealousy come across Chloe's face as she heard Tanner speak about this woman. I felt bad for her.

I smacked Tanner in the gut with the back of my hand and motioned my head toward Chloe. He quickly got the message and immediately began to fawn over her. I smiled to myself.

As I walked past the slack jawed men toward my room to put my dress away, my father caught my attention.

"Karah! Karah come over here please." He waved his hand in a 'come here' fashion.

"Yeah dad, what's up?" I walked over to where my father and the runway model of a party planner he had hired were standing. I had never seen myself as ugly until I stood next to this sun-kissed goddess. "Bitch." I thought to myself. I knew it was unfair, I didn't even know this woman. As my father attempted to show me all the things they had planned out, my attention was led elsewhere when Ryker walked past the woman to retrieve a drink from the fridge. My full attention was snapped back to the party planner when she put her hand on his shoulder and asked his opinion of whatever was in the folder in front of her. I watched and waited for her to take her hand off his shoulder. She didn't. "Yup, she's a bitch." My thoughts grew angrier in my head. I clenched the countertop until I noticed Chloe pulling at my arm.

"Excuse us for just a moment." She gave her best fake smile and proceeded to drag me down the hall. "Seriously? You can't kill the party planner!" she whispered in a hushed tone.

"I know, I know. I can't believe this. I'm getting jealous over a guy who isn't even mine." I rolled my eyes at myself.

"Not that he doesn't want to be." She smiled a wily smile as I pulled her into the open room.

"Spill. NOW." I demanded. I had a grip on both of her shoulders.

"All I'm saying is he has a thing for you. So, stop worrying about party planner Barbie in there." She gave me an eyeroll of her own and looked at me in a placating way.

"Boy, you're just a fountain of information, aren't ya?" I snickered at her attempt to be intimidating.

She laughed. "Come on" She nodded toward the door. "She's fixing to leave anyways."

"Good, then maybe the guys can regain blood flow to their heads ABOVE the belt ine." We both laughed as we came back into the common area. Of course, all the men were still standing around like lovesick puppies. I noticed, with glee, that Ryker was no longer in the room.

The following days were quiet and uneventful. The morning of my birthday, I woke

33

drenched in sweat. I couldn't remember everything about the dream, but just that something had angered me. "What the hell?" I thought. I decided I needed to immediately take a shower. I looked at myself in the mirror and noticed my skin was flushed and I felt a little warmer than usual. I turned on the shower and stepped in. As I did, the water felt frigid and icy. "Seriously?!" I complained. I washed myself as fast as I could just to get out of the glacial water. I quickly dressed in a huff as I wondered what in the world was going on. I decided not to dwell on it and to just go get breakfast.

As I reached the kitchen everyone was there.

"HAPPY BIRTHDAY!" They all screamed at once.

"Fucking hell!" I jumped. I wasn't a fan of loud noises before coffee. "Shut up Christian!" I figured might as well stop him before he started. The room filled with laughter. As I grabbed a cup of coffee, my dad gave me a hug.

"Happy birthday, kiddo. I'm sorry I missed so many of them before." I couldn't stop the tears that began to fill my eyes. I hugged my father tightly, burying my face into his shoulder so that no one could see me cry. He pulled back from me, with concern on his face.

"Karah, you're burning up. Do you feel ok?" The consideration on his face was refreshing.

"Yeah, Dad, I feel fine." I tried to inconspicuously wipe the tears from my face.

"You sure?"

I chuckled, "Yes, Dad, I'm sure."

Hesitantly, my dad conceded. "Well, ok, if you're sure. Oh, and be ready by eight pm."

"Aye aye capi-tan!" I laughed while giving a salute.

After breakfast, I trained. During the training, I became unreasonably tired. I decided it best I lay down for a while before I would have to get ready for the party. I fell asleep quickly but as I did, my nightmares returned.

"Karah! Karah!" Christian shouted, shaking me awake. "Geez, are you ok?!"

"Huh? Wh- what happened?" I was disoriented and trying to get my bearings.

"You were screaming and fighting in your sleep. You're soaked." He quickly pulled me into a hug and held my head to his chest.

"It was just a nightmare...I'm okay, really." I reassured him with a slight squeeze.

Christian looked at me quizzically while he studied my face as if to make sure there wasn't anything, I wasn't telling him.

"Really Christian. I'm fine...you'd think I'd be used to them by now. Wait, what time is it?"

"Six pm. I was coming to wake you up when I heard you screaming." He finally let me go and stood.

"Oh, well, thanks. I guess we should probably start getting ready."

"Yeah, probably. Plus, you stink!" He let out an uproarious laugh. I laughed along with him, as I swung a pillow at his head.

I pushed Christian out the door and took a shower. I did my hair and makeup and donned the black dress. "Shoes." I looked around at the scattered variety on the floor, none seemed to be what I wanted. "Fuck, I forgot shoes. Fuck it." I dug my black low top Converse out of the closet and put them on. "These will just have to do."

As I opened the door to my room, my father, had been waiting for me.

"Wow, kiddo. Look at you. You look stunning." He took my hand and spun me in a circle. "A little lower cut than I would prefer." His tone was one that only a father could perfect.

"But it has pockets." I giggled.

He offered his arm and waited for me to link my arm with his. "Come on. You don't want to be late for your own party, do you?"

"Well, I mean, the party can't start until I get there, right?" I asked cheekily.

"That's my girl." We laughed as he escorted me across the compound to the room he had built specifically for special occasions.

As I prepared myself to enter, I could hear the chatter of the guests and the clinking of glasses. When I walked in the room, an eerie silence fell over it. I immediately began to wonder if my boob had popped out my dress or if I had toilet paper stuck to my shoe. Just as quickly as the room hushed, a chorus of "Happy birthdays!" came from the guests. The room was beautiful. Strings of twinkling lights adorned the ceiling and walls. Deep red satin lined the tables and chairs. A lone disco ball hung in the center of the room, slowly turning.

Chloe and Tanner came sprinting over to me.

"Karah, you look so pretty! Happy birthday!!" Chloe hugged me.

"Yeah Karah, you look hot." Chloe and I shot Tanner a look and started laughing. "What? What's so funny?" He was genuinely confused, and it only made the situation more comical.

"Thanks guys." I was already starting to feel better.

As I made my way through the room, I greeted guests, some of whom I knew, others I had no clue who the hell they were. I finally reached the bar, where Christian was standing with a smile on his face.

"Well look at you birthday girl. You clean up well. And much less smelly." He laughed.

I smacked him in the stomach with the back of my hand and leaned my back against the bar. "Shut up. You don't look too shabby yourself."

He adjusted his lapels in a rather dramatic fashion, with a big grin on his face. "Why, thank you."

"I think I messed up, Christian." His smile quickly faded.

"What do you mean? How?" his voice was filled with concern.

As I looked straight ahead, not making eye contact with my best friend, I replied.

"I think I went and caught feelings for Ryker."

His concern was replaced with relief. He chuckled. "I think if you can get past him being a stubborn pain in the rear, you guys will be great together."

Clay walked up to the bar, closely followed by Desmond.

"Happy birthday, Cara." Clay mentioned, more in passing as he grabbed a beer from the bar.

"Yeah, happy birthday!" Des wrapped me in a friendly hug.

"It's Kar- oh whatever, thank you, Clay. Thanks Des."

As they walk away, I turned to Christian. "He doesn't like me much, does he?" I tilted my head in the direction both men left in.

"Who? Oh, Clay? Nah, it's not that he doesn't like YOU specifically. He just refuses to get close to anyone after what happened to his wife and daughter." He glanced away from me and shifted uncomfortably.

"Clay was married?" I could hear the surprise in my own voice as I tried to get Christian to look back at me.

"Oh, uh, yeah. UMBRA killed his wife when they abducted his daughter. A few days later there was a message left on his machine of his daughter screaming and crying. He tried everything to find her. But you know how the brotherhood is, constantly moving. He never heard from his daughter again. He's convinced she's dead too." He finally met my eyes again and I felt the gravity of his pain for his friend.

After a brief pause, "Oh...wow."

The awkward silence of sadness was broken as Ryker approached.

"Hey Karah. Happy birthday. You look beautiful." He greeted me by planting a quick and gentle kiss on my cheek. His eyes started at my Converse covered feet and slowly perused their way up until he met my eyes with a smirk. I felt my entire face go flush. Christian snorted into his drink. With a threatening glare, he recognized his cue to leave.

"Thanks Ryker. You look...you look...." My brain had a momentary lapse in common word formation as I looked at Ryker. His perfectly tailored, navy blue suit hugged his body flawlessly. It could be seen the amount of time he spent training even through all the layers of clothing covering his muscled body.

"I look what exactly?" The smirk still hadn't left his face, and could I dare say, he was amused?

"Perfect." My mouth had spit the word out before my brain could stop it.

Before Ryker had the chance to say anything else, a waiter dressed as if he were doing his best impersonation of a penguin walked by with a tray offering us both a glass of pink champagne. Rosé. My favorite. The clinking of glasses attracted our attentions to the front of the room where my father stood with his glass raised high to make a toast.

As I listened to my father's speech, I saw Atticus smiling at me from across the room. Behind him, lurked the figure of a man hiding in his shadow. I couldn't see the figure, but I could feel his eyes on me. I tried to shake the feeling of being watched by a shadow and listen to my father. He had finished his toast, and everyone took a drink. I blew my father a kiss. I had to know who the shadow man was and apparently from the look on my face, Ryker knew something was amiss. I made it half-way across the room before the hidden figure stepped into the light, which stopped me dead in my tracks. When I saw his face, the crystal champagne flute slipped from my hand and smashed into thousands of glittering shards on the floor.

"Are you okay?" Ryker whispered into my ear. His eyes on the same person mine were. He put his arm around my waist protectively and drew me slightly closer to his side.

My stomach clenched and knees became weak. I was thankful that Ryker decided to hold me, otherwise I fear I would have stumbled. All the while, I never took my eyes off the man across the room. I knew it was fight or flight. I decided on fight.

"YOU! WHAT THE FUCK ARE YOU DOING HERE?!?! I yelled, as I stormed my way through the crowd towards him, Ryker close behind. I reached him and instinctually slapped him hard across his pale face, leaving a red handprint on his white cheek. His black hair that was once slicked back, fell into his face and his green eyes burned.

Atticus stepped his massive build between us.

"Karah, you must have him mistaken for someone else. This is my brother." He gestured to the man, with nothing but confusion on his face.

"Your what?! Adriel is your BROTHER?!" I took a small step backwards and into Ryker, his hand came to my hip to steady me.

"Uhm…well yes." Atticus looked more confused than a six-year-old trying to do calculus. "How do you know each other?" His head whipped from me to Adriel.

"Oh, your dear brother didn't tell you? He's my ex. Yeah, the manipulative bastard who lied to me for a year!" With that I stormed out of the room, letting my flight reflexes kick in.

Meanwhile back in the room, Atticus looked at his brother Adriel.

"Brother…what did you do?" The disappointment coming from him was palpable.

"I'm guessing this would be a bad time to mention he's moving in, huh?" Tanner asked awkwardly as he scratched the back of his head.

∞Three∞

As I ran from the room, I could hear footsteps following closely behind me.

"Karah! Karah, wait." Ryker called after me.

I only stopped running once I reached the common area and collapsed on the couch like an over-dramatic cartoon princess.

"Karah, are you okay?" Ryker's voice was different than I had ever heard it before. It was soft and protective. He scooped me up into his lap to comfort me. I was in such an emotional state that the gravity of his actions didn't sink in.

"I hate him. I hate him so much. Why did he have to show up here? Tonight, of all nights." I cried and buried my tear-soaked face into his firm chest. His arms tightened slightly, giving me the added comfort, I so desperately needed.

"Shhh. It's okay. I don't know what happened between you two, but it's all going to be okay." He said as he stroked my hair. He put his fingers under my chin and gently raised my face to look at him. "He is never going to hurt you again. I promise."

I could tell by the look on his face, he meant every word. One by one, the residents of the compound trickled in. Most of whom were too stunned by my outburst to say anything.

"Karah, honey, we need to talk." My dad said with a mix of sadness and concern on his face, his hands tucked into his pockets.

I wiped the tears from my eyes and stood to face him. "I'm sorry about that, Dad. I know you were really wanting for me to have a nice birthday." I couldn't help the guilt that was sinking in from my actions. Dad went out of his way to make this night perfect for me, and I ruined it. I felt the anger flare up again. "No," I thought to myself, "this isn't my fault. This is all because of Adriel." I felt my skin heat and I had to take a breath to calm down.

"Oh, honey, this isn't about that. We need to talk about Adriel." He refused to make any attempt at eye contact with me. I could only assume he knew his words would upset me.

I snickered at the asinine words coming from my father's mouth. "No, we really don't."

"Yeah, kiddo we do. He's coming to stay here, just like you did. He's Atticus's brother and he wants to get rid of the brotherhood just as badly as we do." I think he was trying to convince himself more than he was me.

"Really Dad, is that what he told you?" I ran my hand through my hair and shook my head, irritated. I looked back to my father with contempt on my face. "Who do you think caused me to believe that you knew about me the entire time and that you just didn't want me?" I threw my arms outwards. "Who do you think manipulated me for a year after I escaped?" My ire was rising the more I spoke. I let my arms fall as I watched disbelief wash across my father's face.

"Karah, we can't just turn our backs on people just because we don't like them. As much as either of us may not like him." He looked at me pleadingly, his eyes begging me to understand the difficult position he was in.

"Uh, we can, and we should." I retorted sharply. The disgust in my voice was clear as the volume in it began to rise.

"Karah." Suddenly, he had a very stern, father-like tone.

I threw my hands up, defeated. "You know what, fine. Fuck it. Whatever." Atticus and Adriel slowly walked in behind my dad. I locked eyes with Adriel. "But you keep that greasy snake the hell away from me." I may have been speaking to my dad, but I wanted it to be clear to Adriel I wanted nothing to do with him.

I stormed out of the common area and down the hall, slamming my bedroom door as hard as possible. After about a minute of pacing, I heard a light knock on the door.

"Go away!" I didn't know who was on the other side of the door and I wasn't sure I cared.

"Karah, can we talk?" I heard Ryker's voice from the other side of the door.

I sighed. Mostly, from relief and I opened the door. I guess I did care who was on the other side. I found myself glad it was Ryker and no one else. I stepped aside so that he could enter the room. I plopped down on the bed causing the tulle of my dress to poof up like a black satin cloud around me.

"I hate seeing you like this, doll." Ryker said as he took my hand.

"I'm not sure why you care." I snapped. I hadn't realized how cruel the words were until after they came spewing from my mouth. I felt much worse as I watched the hurt sweep across his perfect face. "I'm sorry, Ryker." I felt the fight leave me as my body sagged with the weight of the evening.

"It's okay. You're upset. I get it." His gaze fixated at my hand in his. He turned it over and ran his fingers over the lines in my palm. "Soft," he murmured to himself. I don't think he meant for me to hear it, so I acted like it wasn't said. The heat that ran through my body this time was for a different reason. He cleared his throat and flicked his eyes to my face and quickly away again.

"You do?" My tone softened as my brain registered what he had said.

"Yeah. I do. I care about you." His gaze met mine again, and I held my breath as the next words came from his lips, "I didn't think I would when we met, but I've found myself constantly thinking about you." He seemed almost embarrassed with the confession, which was something I was not used to from him. He was always so confident in his actions.

46

"Really?" My voice had more shock in it than I wanted it to.

Ryker laughed. I had never heard him laugh. It was as perfect as he was, low and husky with just a touch of baritone.

"Yeah, really." Before I had a chance to reply, Ryker leaned his face down and firmly kissed my lips. They were welcoming and softer than I had anticipated. I have wanted nothing more than to be right here with him since the moment I laid my eyes on him. I sucked his lower lip between mine and gently bit down. His tongue danced across my top lip before searching for my own. With a sweeping motion he ran his hands up the back of my neck and tilting it, effectively deepening the kiss. His mouth tasted like the finest whiskey and honey, brewed, and aged to absolute sublimity. My heart fluttered as a tingle ran down my spine. Too soon our perfect kiss was interrupted. Someone had cleared their throat from the doorway, I looked up and saw Adriel standing there. My anger started to rise again because of the audacity this snake had.

"Karah, can I spea- ". Before he could finish his sentence, Ryker had crossed the room, his muscular body tightened and flexed, ready for anything that may happen.

"Leave. Now." Ryker growled through clenched teeth. His wide shoulders blocked Adriel from coming any further into the room.

"I'll leave when she tells me to." Adriel hissed back. I could see the hatred in his eyes as he glared at Ryker.

Tired and annoyed, I walked over to where Ryker was standing, holding the door. Gently I pushed passed him and slammed the door in Adriel's face. I turned to Ryker; the momentary look of confusion on his face was quickly swept away by amusement. I gave him a quick kiss on the lips and walked to the bathroom to change clothes. Moments later, I came out from the bathroom, wearing cotton shorts and an oversized sweatshirt, ready for bed. My beautiful dress laid crumpled in the corner.

"Come lay with me." I told more than asked him, as I pulled away the bedding from one side of the bed, so that he could join me. I watched as Ryker stripped to his boxers, leaving his clothes where they landed and got into bed with me. I laid my head on his chest and listened to his heartbeat, strong and steady beneath my ear. My finger unconsciously traced the thick scar closest to it. His trailed lightly up and down the length of my spine. If it weren't for the exhaustion, I would have taken full advantage of this magnificent, damaged, specimen of a man laying in my bed. I continued to listen to his heart until I fell asleep. For the first night in weeks, there were no nightmares.

The first rays of the autumn sun peaked around the curtains into the room. I laid there and kept my eyes closed. I didn't want this moment with Ryker to end. As we laid in the bed, my head still on his chest, he held my hand. I began to wonder if he was awake until the sudden feeling of being watched came over me once again.

"Ryker?" I whispered in case he was still asleep.

"Yeah, doll?" he replied, reaffirming my paranoid feeling of being watched.

"Stop staring at me, it's creepy." I continued to keep my eyes closed. I felt his chest move when he chuckled to himself.

"We should probably get up." Although he didn't move.

"Ugggggghhh...I don't ever want to leave this bed." I groaned.

"You win." He laughed. "We'll just stay here forever." He tightened the arm he had draped over my waist.

I snuggled closer to him and took a deep breath, inhaling his scent. "God, he smells amazing." I said to myself. The smell of an earthy sandalwood filled my nose, giving me a sense of comfort, I had never experienced before, and I forgot the spectacle from the previous night.

"Sounds like a plan to me." I smiled as I replied. A knock came from the door.

"Noooooooo." I whimpered, as I buried my face into his chest. "Maybe if we stay quiet, they'll leave." I said hopefully. The knock came again.

"Want me to get it?" Ryker asked me as he ran his hand through my hair.

"Ugh. I guess." I said grumpily.

Ryker was swift in his movements, he got out of the bed, and quickly slid his pants on and walked to the door. As he opened it, he seemed relieved that it was Atticus and not Adriel who knocked.

"Hey, Atticus." Ryker yawned and stretched as he opened the door.

"Oh, uhm, hello Ryker. I assume Karah is somewhere in there?" Atticus replied, surprised to see Ryker open the door.

"Hey, Atticus. What can I do for you?" I asked as I finally climbed out of the bed. I walked up behind Ryker and wrapped my arms around his sides and up to his shoulders.

"Can we talk for a moment?" he questioned hesitantly. His voice resembled a child preparing to ask a parent for something they knew they wouldn't get.

I felt Ryker's body tense. I kissed the back of his shoulder as to ease his worries.

"Yeah, give me a minute okay?" I told Atticus.

Ryker turned to look at me. "It's fine. I promise" I whispered. He gathered the rest of his clothes from the floor, tapped the end of my nose with his finger and gave me a quick kiss on the cheek before he walked out the door.

"What's up, Atti?" I moved from the door, allowing him to enter the room.

"I wanted to discuss my brother." His eyes wouldn't meet mine as he continuously glanced around the room.

"Then you know where the door is." I pointed to the door with the other hand on my hip. "I don't want to talk to him or about him." I crossed my arms across my chest and raised an eyebrow at him.

"Please, Karah. He's not the monster you think he is." His voice was pleading. I knew he wanted to believe his brother was a good man. Maybe he was in a past life. But the Adriel I knew was nothing more than a monster.

"And that is supposed to give me back the year I wasted on him?" I retorted coldly.

"I suppose not. But it could give you a chance to start over fresh." I felt bad for Atticus having to come to his brother's defense.

"Nope! Byyyyye." I said as I attempted to push the red oak tree of a man back out through the door he entered in. Why did I think I could budge him, again?

"Just talk to him, Karah." He begged as he allowed me to push his massive frame.

"Nope!" I slammed the door. "Fucking hell." I flopped back onto my bed.

I took a moment before I got ready for the day. I had no urge to face anyone apart from Ryker. Reluctantly, I dressed. I knew I couldn't hide out in my room all day. However, another side of me really wanted to try. I was already emotionally exhausted, and the day had just begun. I laid back across the bed and let out a heavy sigh. Just then, the door swung open, hitting the wall behind it. I sat up to see who would barge into my room without knocking first. In the doorway, stood Adriel. His black shoulder length hair was once again slicked back. His green eyes were bright with a mixture of emotions I didn't recognize on him. His thin lips were pursed. As I looked at him, stunned that he would even have the audacity to show his face around me. His face...his face was one of the reasons I had fallen in love with him so many years ago. He looked as if he had been carved by Michelangelo from the purest white marble. He walked into the room. Reality rejoined the party and I bolted from the bed.

"What the actual fuck? Didn't I tell you to stay the fuck away from me?!" I could feel my anger rising again and I felt the flush over my skin.

He took another step closer to me. "I missed you my darling." His voice was sticky, and his words clung in the air.

"Did you miss the part where I said leave me alone? Clearly, I didn't slap you hard enough to get the point across." I knew how harsh my words were. This time I meant it that way.

"My sweet Karah." He took yet another step closer to me. He had come close enough I could smell him. The smell of musk and leather. "Oh, how I have missed you." He smiled, looking every bit as slimy as I'd seen him numerous times before.

"Tough titty. Now leave." was once again pointing to the door.

In one prompt motion, his hands were cupping my face. They were cold and demanding compared to Ryker's.

"I've missed you." He repeated. Taking a deep breath in, as though he wanted to keep my scent alive in his memory. As swiftly as he held my face, he kissed me. It was hard and angry, filled with raw, primal lust. I shoved him away with both hands as hard as I could which caused him to slam into the dresser behind him.

"How fucking DARE you!" I exclaimed. I could feel as my emotions began to get the better of me. "How dare you come here after everything you put me through!" I pointed an accusing finger at him. "How dare you have the gall to speak to me. How dare you fucking touch me!" My breathing had become ragged and uneven, my chest heaving with every word.

"Karah, I still love you." He seemed unconvinced of the words I had just said. He tried to move toward me again, but my next words stopped his advance.

"YOU NEVER LOVED ME! I was a TOY to you! THAT'S the problem! I LOVED YOU! I LOVED YOU AND YOU BROKE ME!!!!" I yelled. The anger I had spread through me and made my entire body hot. From the corner of my eye, I could see the group had gathered by the door.

"Uhhhhhh, guys." Tanner had become audibly frightened, letting the quiver in his voice come out. "Guys, what's happening to her eyes?!"

"Oh fuck!" I heard Desmond say in full shock. His cocoa skin had gone pale.

I glanced at the mirror on the other side of the room. My eyes had turned from a golden amber to red. A bright scarlet red. My fists were clenched so tightly I felt like I punctured the skin with my nails, turning as hot as my hatred for the man standing in front of me.

"Uhhhhm...Is she on fire?" Clay was unreasonably calm considering what had occurred. I looked down at my hands. There were flames dancing across them. Shocked, I unclenched my fists. As I looked up, I saw a blur and then Adriel flew across the room and smashed into the mirror. The glass fell around his body as he landed. Ryker had run in, putting his speed and strength through his shoulder directly into Adriel. I had never seen that type of rage on Ryker's face before. I was terrified and at the same time oddly turned on by it.

"Ryker!" My dad, Atticus, and Christian all shouted in concert.

"I warned him." He was shaking with his rage. "I warned him yesterday to stay away from her. Look what he did to her!" Ryker shouted as he motioned to me. My anger was replaced by the overwhelming feeling of safety. As my feelings shifted, the flames on my hands died out. I glanced back at the shards of broken mirror; my eyes had returned to normal. Atticus rushed to Adriel's side, helping him off the floor and out of the pile of shattered glass. Ryker's attention went back to Adriel.

"I told you to stay away from her." He was clenching and unclenching his hands at his sides. "Next time I won't just knock you on your ass." He said and revolved his focus back to me as he walked over. He reached for my hands. Out of fear I pulled away from him. Not fear of him. Fear FOR him. I had no idea what these new powers were or where they came from. Or how to control them.

"I don't want to burn you." I whispered as I stared at my hands.

"I don't care." He took my hand in his and gave it a slight squeeze.

My dad hurried into the room as Atticus and the others helped Adriel limp out.

"Ryker, you have got to keep yourself in check." Apparently, I wasn't the only one my father would use his 'dad voice' on.

"Dad, Adriel crossed a line!" I tried to defend Ryker, but he spoke before I could continue.

"Listen, Thomas, if that piece of shit is going to be staying, you had better believe I will be here to protect Karah from him. From anything, from ANYONE. I will always protect her." He said as he intertwined his fingers with mine.

"Whatever THIS is..." my dad said as he motioned at Ryker and my interlocked hands. "...it will not interfere with work. Got it?" His stern tone conveyed his seriousness. He made eye contact with me," And Karah, Reed needs to see you in the lab." He pinched the bridge of his nose as he remarked, almost to himself, "And clearly, we're going to have to up your sessions with Marcus." He spun on his heel and walked out.

After a moment of silence, I looked up at Ryker. "You know, he raises a good point. What is this between us exactly?"

"Isn't it obvious? You're my girl." With a smile as he tugged me towards him wrapping me in his strong arms and kissed me. Contradictory to Adriel's kiss, Ryker's was passionate and strong but kind.

We finally pried ourselves apart from each other. I took a second to catch my breath.

"Your girl, huh?" I asked sheepishly.

"Yup." He smiled and wrapped his strapping arm around my shoulders. As we walked out of my room, Chloe stood there waiting for me to come out.

"I have to go run some errands. I'll see you tonight." Ryker said with a quick kiss and walked away.

"Heeeeeey." She was cautious with her approach.

"Hey, Chloe." I greeted her with a little wave.

"You, uh, you feeling okay? You kind of went all rawr." She did her best imitation of a dinosaur. Maybe it was a lion. I couldn't really tell, anything intimidating coming from her was always quite the opposite.

"Yep. I'm fantastic. I'm heading to the lab now. Walk with me?" I gestured down the hallway in the direction of the lab.

"Of course. So...told you he had a thing for you!" Excitedly, she nudged me in the side with her elbow.

"Shaddup!" I laughed as we approached Uncle Reed's lab.

"Well, I have to go let Tanner know you're okay. Everything kind of freaked him out a little bit." She said as she held her forefinger and thumb a few inches apart.

"Tell him I'm okay." I hugged Chloe and she skipped away as I walked into the lab. It was impressive. I didn't know much about science or anything related to the work Uncle Reed did in there, but I could tell an abundance of the equipment had to have a hefty price tag on it.

"Hey, Uncle Reed."

"Hey Karah. Have a seat." He pointed at the chair next to his desk. "How are you feeling?" He asked as he started getting the equipment he would need together.

"I'm okay I guess." I shrugged as I sat in the hard metal chair.

"Let's start by taking your temperature. Lift your tongue." He put the thermometer in my mouth. After a few seconds, the thermometer beeped. "Hmm…103.4°." We spent the next hour or so together as he drew blood, ran tests, and repeatedly mumbled to himself.

"I think the powers could either be triggered by your body trying to fight off the mutations, causing your cells to release more powers or they're dormant powers that could be triggered by stress. I'm not sure yet. I'll know more after I finish running these tests." He told me as he started to remove his gloves and clean the space we used.

"So anytime I'm stressed, I'll get a new power? Gee, that's fabulous." There was an excessive amount of sarcasm dripping from my words.

"Honestly, I don't know. I haven't seen this before in any of the others." His brow furrowed as he started to think of all he would have to do.

"Oh...goodie." I sighed, defeated.

I left the lab wondering about the possibilities and what other changes I would go through. As I was leaving, Nova was coming out of the training room.

"Hey, Nova." I acknowledged her as she started walking the same direction towards the common area.

"Oh, hey. I've been meaning to ask you about something, but things always seem to be going wrong." She stopped in the middle of the hall and I had no choice but to stop as well.

"Okay, shoot. What's up?" Suddenly, I was very curious what Nova had to ask.

"You and Christian are close. What's his deal?" She tried to sound uninterested, but I could hear the genuine curiosity in her voice.

"What do you mean?" I asked slightly confused but really, I just wanted her to put her big girl panties on and say it.

"Does uh, does he have a girlfriend outside the compound?" she asked in a lower voice than her normal speaking volume.

I looked at her slyly. "You liiiiiiike him!"

"I- I, well I might. Maybe." She tried her best to act nonchalant.

59

I raised an eyebrow at her and smirked. "Want me to talk to him for you?"

"No. No, just see if he is interested." She shook her head and tried to tuck some of her hair behind her ear. Seeing her uncharacteristically nervous warmed my heart towards her even more.

"Dude, literally the same thing." I laughed as I walked away.

After Nova's revelation, I immediately went to find Christian. He deserved to be with someone that would make him happy. And luckily, Nova was the opposite of his airhead of an ex. I couldn't stand her. I was glad when they broke up and I made it a point to tell him. I wanted him to be happy and I knew that dingbat didn't have the capabilities to do that.

"Hey Clay, have you seen Christian?" I asked as I passed the couch where he was stretched out. He only responded by pointing towards the hallway. "Bedroom, gotcha." I learned that it was easier to ignore his disdain for people.

I stuck my head in his room around the doorframe and lightly knocked. Christian was sitting at his computer desk.

"Hey buuuuuuddy." I greeted him in the way I usually did when I wanted something.

"Uh-oh, what do you need?" His gaze broke from his computer screen and he looked up at me.

I entered his room and plopped on his bed like a child. "Just want to talk to my brother."

"About? Please tell me it's not about Ryker. You two just started." His voice had a hint of disappointment as he crossed his arms over his chest.

"No, no, this isn't about me and Ryker. It's about you and Nova." I mirrored his pose.

"Me and Nova?!" He was honestly startled. "What do you mean?" For once, I had him genuinely confused.

"Is there anything there? Or do you think maybe there could be? Like, does she give you butterflies?" I asked, jokingly.

His faced flashed a light pink. "It doesn't really matter she wouldn't be interested in me anyways." He said uncomfortably.

The ridiculous statement that came from him caused me to throw a well-aimed pillow at the back of his head.

"Hey! What was that for?!" He said loudly as he rubbed the back of his head.

"Do you seriously think I would drag my ass in here and bring her up, if she weren't interested? Don't be naïve. You're not stupid." scoffed and raised my eyebrow at him.

"Wait, did she say something to you?" His eyes lit up and he sat forward in his chair. Apparently, that got his attention.

"Duh!" I rolled my eyes saying. "Don't be a chicken-shit. Go talk to her." I gestured towards the door.

"You really do curse like a sailor, don't you?" He laughed at his own question he so obviously already knew the answer.

"Meh." I shrugged my shoulders. "Part of my charm." I added with a less than convincing smile. "Now, I have to go find my dad and let him know what Uncle Reed said."

"Oh yeah, how did that go?"

"I'll probably end up turning into a dragon by the time I'm fifty." I said as I walked out and left him with a dumbfounded look on his face.

∞Four∞

I walked to my dad's office. I approached the large wooden door and saw him with his elbow on the desk, his hand held his forehead. He looked more stressed than I had ever seen him. It was out of character for him to look like that.

"Hey dad. Everything okay?" I asked as I stepped into his office and stood in front of the great mahogany desk.

"Huh? Oh, hey kiddo. I think we need to talk." He said as he looked up at me.

"Listen, Dad, if this is about Adriel or Ryker, I really don't want to have this conversation." I shook my hand, dismissively. I didn't need to talk guys with my father. Ever.

"No, it's not about either of them, although, we do need to discuss them as well. This is about the past." He rubbed his chin, full of worry.

"The past? What about it?" I hated talking about my past. I always tried to keep it buried. It was a time in my life that was so dark and lonely that I'd rather just forget about it altogether.

"About MY past." He paused. "Adriel wasn't COMPLETELY wrong."

"I don't like where this is headed, Dad." I took a small step back from my father's cesk.

"I had the suspicion your mother may have been pregnant the last time I spoke to her." He dropped his gaze from mine briefly before bringing it back to me. "But I didn't know for sure. But then again, I also never asked her about it, either."

"So, you knew? You knew I was out there, and you never came to find me?" I couldn't hide the hurt in my voice as I took yet another step away from him.

"I didn't know. Not for sure. Not until Adriel came to me saying he suspected his new girlfriend to be my daughter. I still have no idea how he knew." He was starting to gesture with his hands, which was something I haven't seen him do before. "I guess he thought I knew and didn't care because I didn't take him for his word. I'm so sorry honey." He said as he rose from his desk and walked around it to me. He tried to hug me.

"I can't do this right now." With both of my hands held up, I pulled away from him and rushed out the door. I just wanted to get away as fast as possible. Rather than running to my room where people could bother me, I bolted for the front door. I had to get away. Away from my dad. From Adriel. From all the questions. My head reeled from my father's confession.

A few hours later I found myself wandering around Times Square. I had been so engrossed in the thoughts in my head, I had no idea where I was going or where I had been. I was lost. The sun had already begun to set, and the city's nightlife started to kick up.

"Fuck." I said to myself. "This can't be happening." I turned the corner to walk down another street that I wouldn't remember. I caught in my peripheral vision two sleazy looking men who kept their eyes glued to me. I crossed the busy street, hoping it was just my own paranoia. They crossed as I did.

"Maybe I can get through this alleyway and they'll lose interest." I thought. I knew it was a terrible plan, making myself more secluded away from lights and people. I watched enough horror flicks to know better. But no, I did it anyway. I grabbed my phone from my back pocket and immediately dialed Christian's number.

"Please pick up, please pick up." I said out loud. I looked behind me to see if the men had followed me. Only one man stood behind me.

"Don't worry about calling anyone, sweet cheeks, we'll take you anywhere you need to go." The man said, sneering and grabbed for my phone. It fell hard to the concrete below.

"How about this? I go on my way and you go to hell? Hmm? Sound good to you, dickhead?" This is it. I knew my mouth would get me killed one day. At that moment, the second man grabbed me from behind, holding me firmly in place by pulling my upper arms back. I told myself not to stress in case the powers were, in fact, stress induced.

"I could cut that nasty tongue right out of your pretty little mouth." The man in front of me was surprisingly menacing considering his rat like features. The switchblade in his hand shot out with a click as he stepped forward.

"Don't stress. Don't stress. Don't stress." I kept repeating in my head, as he ran the end of the cold steel from the knife down my cheek. He pressed the knife against my throat, and I could feel the blade cut through my skin, and a trickle of blood slid down my neck. "Okay, I'm stressed."

I felt my eyes roll to the back of my head and everything went black.

When I woke up, I was in a hospital bed. I could hear the heart monitor beeping rhythmically. Ryker was by my side holding my hand in his and had his head rested on the back of it.

"Hey there, soldier boy." My voice was hoarse and came out barely above a whisper. I had never heard myself sound like that. Ryker's head snapped up with enough speed I thought he would break his neck.

"Hey there doll." A relieved smile took over where his anxious expression previously was. He reached one hand up and stroked the side of my face while he kept the other hand firmly in place, holding mine. "I'll be right back." He said and kissed the back of my hand where he had been holding it. He went to the door and I saw him motion to someone in the waiting room. He came back to his place at my bedside, quickly followed by Christian and my dad.

"Karah! Thank god you're awake." My dad was full of relief, with tears in his eyes.

"What the hell happened? How long have I been here?" I was still groggy and not completely convinced I was awake.

"It's been three days since I found you in the alley, Karah. We were kind of hoping YOU could tell US what happened." Christian was standing at the foot of the bed.

"Three days? Well, that sucks. Did I miss anything important?" I asked as I attempted to sit up in the bed. Ryker put his arm behind my back and raised the head of the bed. I gave him an appreciative look as I got situated.

"Just that when I found you there were two dead guys with no hearts." Christian's traditionally chipper face now had concern etched deep on it.

My eyes grew wide. "Well, that's an unexpected turn of events. Your guess is as good as mine."

"Karah, what's the last thing you remember?" Ryker asked as he took my hand again.

I recounted the story of how I ended up in the alley. The two men. Everything that occurred up until the blackout. Ryker's grip on my hand tightened.

"Reed filled me in on his thoughts about your new powers. He tested your cells and when they were put under stressful conditions, they changed. He's confident that your body momentarily evolves to protect yourself from the stress." My dad wiped the tears that had finally fallen, from his face.

"Oh great, so I have the WORST coping mechanism EVER." Which caused my dad, Christian, and Ryker to all give an exhausted laugh. "So, when can I get the hell out of here and go home?" I asked with my free hand on my forehead before I dropped it.

"I'll go talk to the doctor now, kiddo." Dad kissed my forehead and walked away.

Christian turned to Ryker. "Why don't you go home take a shower, get some food and get some rest. I'll call you if anything else happens."

"No. I'm going to stay. But I will go get a cup of coffee." Ryker replied, with a knowing glance towards me.

"Ooo, coffee." I perked up.

"Coming right up." He smiled lightly as he stood and gently kissed my lips as if I were going to break if he kissed me too hard. He walked out and left Christian and I alone in the room.

Christian walked around from the foot of the bed and sat down where Ryker had been sitting.

"How long has he been here?" I asked Christian as I simultaneously nodded toward the door Ryker just walked out of.

"Are you kidding me?" He laughed. "He hasn't left your side except to go to the bathroom. He even asked the nurse for a catheter just so he wouldn't have to get up at all. They didn't go for it, but he tried." His shoulders shook with his mirth.

"That man is something else." I casually shook my head with a weak smile.

"Yeah. I'm pretty sure he's moved past just having feelings for you and is in full blown love with you. How are you feeling by the way?"

"Speaking of love, have you talked to Nova yet?" I know I was trying to avoid the topic. I always felt a sense of shame when I was hurt or sick. I felt like I was weak even though I was anything but.

"No, now don't try to change the subject. How are you feeling? And don't just say you're fine." He said sternly. Giving me his look that he always does when he won't let me get away with anything.

"Honestly? Like I went nine rounds in a no-holds barred boxing match with Atticus. Everything hurts. But please don't make a fuss about it. I just want to go home and if I bitch about it, they'll make me stay longer." I pleaded.

"You're killing me. You're aware of that, right?" he said, disheartened. Ryker returned with three cups of coffee. He handed one to Christian and one to me.

"Mmmmm. Even hospital coffee is better than no coffee." I breathed in the aroma of the stale and slightly burnt excuse for coffee. It may have been crappy, but I appreciated it regardless. "You spoil me." I looked to Ryker, forcing a smile while the muscles in my face screamed in pain.

"Anything for you, babe." The sweet smile on his face may have given proof to Christian's earlier statement of him being in love with me.

"You two are disgusting...adorable but disgusting." Christian said with a playfully appalled look on his face, which caused Ryker and I to laugh making it feel like someone had hit me with a baseball bat in the ribcage.

I saw my father walk past the window with a man in a white coat. They both entered the room. The man was heavy-set with white hair and a bushy mustache that I'm sure caught a lot of the food he seemed to eat.

"I'm Dr. Carson." The doctor began to flip through the medical chart he was holding. "How are you feeling, Karah?" He looked up from the chart over to me.

"I feel fine." Christian shot me a disappointed look, which I returned with my own slight glare, telling him to keep his mouth closed. "When can I get out of here, Doc?" I looked back to the stout man with, what I hoped was, a believable smile.

"I see no reason you can't go home now. Just take it easy for the next couple of days." Dr. Carson said to me with a look in his eyes that said he wasn't falling for my act.

"Will do, Doc." I nodded my head in my attempt to be convincing that I was feeling okay.

"I'll make sure she rests." Ryker looked from me back to him and shook Dr. Carson's hand. "Thank you."

Dr. Carson turned to my dad, "If she blacks out again in the next forty-eight hours, bring her in immediately."

"We will. Thank you." He shook Dr. Carson's hand as well.

"I'll go grab your discharge papers." Then Dr. Carson walked out.

As Dr. Carson walked out, I felt a cool breeze across me, and I noticed I was in a thin hospital gown. "Hey, uhm, where are my clothes and phone?"

"Your clothes had to be cut off, but I grabbed you some from the compound." Christian handed me my clothes from the table next to him. "Your phone is smashed, but your dad has a new one waiting for you. We'll let you get changed." All three men, walked to the door, my dad closed the blinds and pulled it closed behind them.

I sat up slowly. "Fuck." I groaned with a grimace. It took longer for me to get dressed than normal. Every move felt like someone had stabbed very dull, red-hot needles directly into my every muscle. Bruises covered my body, black and purple splotches that looked deep in the tissue. After finally getting my clothes on, I sat hunched at the side of the bed. When a knock came from the door.

"You dressed?" my dad asked. "We have your discharge papers and Christian is getting the car."

"Yeah, Dad. I'm good." I was breathless from the amount of energy it had taken just to get dressed.

He opened the door and him and Ryker entered.

"Let's get you home." Dad said as he held his hand out to help me off the bed.

I tried to walk as straight and as normally as possible. It took more strength than I was used to using. Luckily, Ryker had his arm around my waist in such a way to make sure I wouldn't black out again and fall. After what seemed like hours, we arrived back at the compound and Ryker escorted me inside.

"Can I stay in your room for a little bit?" I asked him when we turned toward the hall.

"Of course. It'll make it easier for me to take care of you that way." He smiled at the idea of me staying in his room with him.

Chloe came running up to me, tears in her eyes.

"Oh my god, Karah! You had us so worried!" she cried and threw her arms around me. Her well-meant intentions caused me to wince and I sucked in air through clenched teeth.

"Are you sure you're okay, doll?" Ryker asked, his disquiet returning to his beautiful face.

"Yup." I strained.

"Oh god! I'm sorry!" Chloe exclaimed as she dropped her arms and stepped away from me.

"I'm just gonna go lay down now." I pointed toward the doorway and attempted to shuffle toward the hall.

"Nope. Come here." Ryker said as he scooped me up in a bridal carry and started towards the hallway.

"Just don't hit my head on the doorframe." I smiled weakly and wrapped my feeble arms around his neck.

"Never." He returned my smile and pressed a light kiss to my forehead.

Once we got to Ryker's room, he laid me gently on the bed.

"Do you need anything?" He asked after he got me settled.

"A shower would be great. I feel disgusting." I ran a hand through my hair with a mildly disgusted look on my face.

"Hmm. How about a bath? That way you don't have to use your strength just to stand." He suggested.

"That works."

"Do, uh, do you want me to help you?" It seemed like he was almost nervous as he shifted his weight from foot to foot.

"Would you really give me any other choice?" I answered his question with my own, with amusement. Seeing him this way was refreshing, showing me that he respected my comfort in the situation.

Ryker stopped for a moment and shook his head. "Nope."

"I guess that settles that."

He helped me to my feet, took me by the hand and lead me to the bathroom where he sat me on the closed toilet.

"Stay. Put." He said with a finger pointed in my direction. "I'm just going to run the bath. How hot do you want the water?" He turned to start filling the tub.

"I want the devil himself to come from the faucet and lick my skin." Apparently, my comment caught him off guard because he stopped dead in his tracks and looked at me with a smile on his face.

"You are SO weird." He laughed with a shake of his head.

I rolled my eyes playfully. "It's part of my charm."

After scarcely any time, the tub was full of steaming water.

"Alright. Arms up." He said as though I were a child.

I complied. He continued to strip my clothes from my body. It wasn't until I stood up, stark naked, that he noticed the bruises that covered me. His eyes darted from the bruises to my eyes. I looked away, ashamed that the first time I was nude in front of him, I looked so broken. For the first time, I watched the tears well up in his blue crystalline eyes and he hit his knees with his head hung.

"Ryker?! Ryker what's wrong?!" I promptly dropped to my knees, ignoring the searing pain radiating throughout my body. I took his head in my hands and raised his face to mine. "Ryker?"

"I'm sorry, Karah. I'm so sorry." Tears spilled from his eyes.

"For what? You didn't do anything." I dipped my head and tried to get him to look at me.

"That's the problem. I didn't do anything. I wasn't there. I promised to protect you and to keep you safe and I wasn't there." The hurt in his voice caught me off guard. This strong, indestructible man in front of me was so worried for me that he let his emotions come out.

"Oh. Oh Ryker, no." I wrapped my arms and pulled him to me. "It's not your fault. None of this was your fault. I'll be okay. I promise." I pulled back and looked into his eyes again.

He looked at me with reassurance on his face. And smiled the sweetest smile.

"I would kiss you right now," his eyes dropped to my lips, "but uhm, you're naked and I don't think I'd be able to stop myself from taking you to my bed and fucking you." His voice turned husky and his eyes darkened with need as he said the last words. I felt a tightening in my core and a rush of adrenaline through my body. This man was going to unglue me and put me back together in the most memorable of ways.

The thought of that, brought a smile across my face that resembled a child being let loose in a candy store.

"Alright, in the tub, doll." He helped me up from the floor, walked me over to the tub and helped me lower myself into the water. The heat instantly soothed my aching body. I let out a very audible sigh. "Better?"

"Very much so." I was content.

After about thirty minutes of Ryker and I talking, the water began to get cold and he helped me from the tub and into a towel.

"Are you feeling any better?" He asked as he tightened the towel around me.

"Yeah, that definitely helped."

"Do you want me to grab you some clothes from your room? I can't lay next to you like that. I wouldn't be able to keep my hands off you." His hand tightened and loosened on the towel like he wasn't sure if he wanted to leave me covered or not.

"I wouldn't complain." I looked up at him through my lashes and bit my lower lip. His eyes zeroed in on that movement and his breath caught.

He was quiet for a moment. Contemplating the possibilities and visibly arguing with himself in his head.

He gently shook his head. "No, doll. Not tonight. Not while you're hurting." He dropped his hands from my towel and took the smallest of steps away from me.

"Okay." There was slightly more disappointment in my voice than I anticipated. "Can I just borrow one of your shirts?" I asked him hopefully, because let's be honest, the man smelled like absolute heaven.

"Of course. Anything for you." His lips spread slight into a smirk. I was sure he knew exactly why I wanted his clothes.

"Well, not ANYTHING." I joked.

"Soon, doll. Soon." His tone was softer as he removed the shirt he was wearing. "Don't you worry your pretty little head about that." He slid his long-sleeved tee-shirt over my head. The end of the shirt stopped just below my ass. Ryker stepped back. "Damn you're gorgeous." He said as his eyes roamed over my body. He licked his bottom lip and gave his head a slight shake. "Come on, in the bed."

"Yes sir." I replied with a smile. I gave him a quick kiss as I walked past him to get in the bed.

We climbed in the plush bed and I took my position with my head laid on his chest.

"Why did you run the other day?" He asked as he ran his fingers through my still wet hair.

I had completely forgotten the events that led me to be in the city that day. I told Ryker the confessions of my father.

"Are you angry with him?" I think he was wondering if he should be angry with my father as well.

"I was. At first. But now I can't help but think that it was what was meant to happen. I had to find my father on my own. Honestly, I probably wouldn't have believed him if he had shown up anyways."

His fingers in my hair stalled once again. "What about Adriel?"

I scoffed. "What about him?"

"Are you still angry with him?" His fingers resumed their movements.

I looked up at Ryker, slightly annoyed. "Yeah, yeah, I'm still mad at him. A little less now than before but still angry. My father isn't the only thing he lied about or did to make me hate him."

Ryker's body tensed. "What'd he do?" He looked from the ceiling and down to me. "Tell me." He urged gently.

"Oh, absolutely not." I shook my head. "No. You don't need another reason to want to kill him." I said as I snuggled back to the warmth of his chest.

The next forty-eight hours were hours of pure bliss. I learned as much as I could about him. From his childhood to how he felt about the people in the compound.

∞Five∞

A week after I came home from the hospital was irritating to say the least. I wanted nothing more than to get back to training. Once I mastered my powers, I could join the others in taking down UMBRA. Unfortunately, I was far from being ready to go out on missions. I had a new power and apparently gained the ability to impersonate a fainting goat and pass out when stressed. Uncle Reed worked tirelessly to find out what caused the black out while Christian and my dad tried to find out what happened to the men that attacked me in the alley. Clay, Des, and Chloe went on a mission to try to find the location of one of the UMBRA facilities. Ryker stayed close to the compound and to me. He never strayed far out of fear of that I would fall unconscious again.

Christian went into the city, to the alley where he found me the previous week in his efforts to find out what occurred at the time I lost consciousness. The shells of what were once my attackers had been removed. After searching the alley, Christian found a small business that had security cameras pointing directly into the alleyway. After some convincing and around three-thousand dollars, he was able to retrieve the footage from the security camera, promptly bringing it to my father at the compound. My father, Christian, Ryker, Uncle

Reed and myself gathered in my father's office to watch the tape.

"Anyone bring popcorn?" I joked as my father put the disc in his computer. "No? Alright." I shrugged.

The screen filled with static and blinked into black and white focus. The office was silent as we watched the incident unfold. As the video showed the men in their attack, Ryker shifted his weight and his body stiffened. The moment had arrived when my eyes rolled and my black out began. However, the video didn't show me collapse as I had originally suspected. Instead, my eyes shifted back to my face, completely black. My body began to lift from the ground which caused the men to fall backwards. I grabbed the man with the knife and lifted him by his collar. As I lowered my face to the man's, my hand shot into his chest, ripping his heart from his body. As this occurred, the second man began to swing a pipe that had been discarded in the alley. The bruises that covered me ached as I watched the pipe connect with my body over and over. I turned my attention to the man behind me. I couldn't recognize the monster on the screen. I rushed the man with ferocity ripping his chest apart. What occurred next made my stomach turn. I released a blood-curdling siren-like scream and ate the men's hearts. My body collapsed in a heap to the ground.

"I think I'm going to be sick." I wrapped my arms across my stomach, watching myself on that video made me physically nauseous. All the men were staring at me in utter disbelief.

"Hmm." Uncle Reed said, taking a small step back.

"I, uh, uhm...well damn." Came from Christian, who I have never heard say a swear word.

My father stayed silent.

"I have to get away from this." I pointed at the screen and rushed from the office. Ryker was by my side as I left the office.

"Karah. Doll, wait." He lightly grabbed my wrist as I attempted to hurry away from my father's office.

"What Ryker? You saw that tape. I'm a monster!" I ripped my hand away from him for fear that I would somehow hurt him right at that moment.

"If you're a monster then you're my monster." He took my hand in his, his eyes met mine and he smirked, "I love you regardless."

My brain almost missed it completely. He said it. He said the words I had been longing to hear.

"You love me?" I was surprised. Christian had mentioned it, and Rykers actions up until this moment all but proved it, but it still caught me off guard. I looked away from him momentarily to get my brain to catch up with his words.

"Yeah, I love you, my little monster." When I looked back at him, a smile had come across his beautiful face. "My little heartbreaker."

"Oh, so we're joking about this already?" I laughed out. "I love you too, Ryker." I said as I put my head into his chest, not want'ng him to see the blush that had crept onto my cheeks.

I hadn't even noticed my dad had walked out from his office until he cleared his throat.

"How are you handling this, Karah?"

I looked at Ryker and then back to my dad. "I think I'm going to be okay. Can you call Marcus? I have to get this under control."

"You got it, kiddo." He remarked with a nod as he pulled his phone from his pocket.

Once everyone had returned to the compound and gathered in the common area, my father explained what had taken place. Reed explained his findings from the tests he had been running.

"Essentially, it's a biological defense mechanism. We had been under the impression that she was developing multiple powers. But it's one power. One power that gives her multiple abilities. You see, her body evolves under immense stress, when the stressor is no longer a threat, her natural state returns." Uncle Reed finished his explanation and swept his gaze over the group.

From the back of the room, Tanner grew very excited. "She needs a badass nickname now!!" He practically yelled as he looked at me expectantly. I shook my head at him and turned my attention back to Uncle Reed.

"Why did I black out this time but not before?" I was confused. When I caught on fire, I was completely lucid, but when that creature came out, I had no recollection of the events.

Uncle Reed pointed a finger at me. "That one I still don't know. But I believe that once the ability presents itself, you can use it by concentrating on that one particular skill."

I thought for a moment. "Which is why we thought I only had that one original power." It was all starting to make sense, but that didn't mean that I completely understood the depths that my power went.

"Exactly. You thought that you only had the one ability, so you only concentrated on that ability." Uncle Reed hooked his thumbs in his front belt loops and leaned against the arm of the couch.

"Moral of the story, let's not stress out Karah until she can learn to control her emotions." My dad had locked eyes with Adriel. I may have been imagining it, but I thought I saw an underlying smirk on his face as he looked in my direction.

After the group chatted for a while, many of them dispersed to debrief from their last mission, train, or went to do their own thing. Nova, Christian, Tanner, Ryker, and I all remained on the couch.

"So, did you two talk yet or am I going to have to beat you both?" I questioned, as I pointed from Christian to Nova and back to Christian.

"Yeah...yeah, we talked." Christian was steadily avoided making eye contact with me.

"Okay, aaaaaand?!" I replied, excitedly.

Christian smiled, wrapping his arm around Nova and pulling her in close to him.

"Thank fucking god! It's about damn time!" I laughed and raised my arms victoriously.

"Hey guys, I want to do something for Chloe's birthday. What do you guys think?" Tanner asked as he looked around to make sure Chloe wasn't anywhere near us.

"For starters don't bring her ex-boyfriend to live with us." I said flatly, which caused a light and rather awkward laughter from my companions. "We can always throw her a party. Just nothing formal. She hates formality."

"OH! We can rent a Dippin Dots cart!" Nova exclaimed.

"I'll see if Dad can hire a party planner...just not the same one he hired for mine." There was a touch of annoyance in my voice at the thought of the tanned beauty that had been here previously.

Ryker let out a snort like chuckle.

"Shut it, buster." I grinned and planted a kiss on his lips.

"Yes ma'am." He laughed as he put an arm on the back of the couch behind me.

"I'm starving, let's go get something to eat." I suggested. We all rose from the couch.

"Yeah, since we're all out of hearts." Christian quipped, letting out a roar of laughter. Which earned him a much-deserved punch to each arm from me and Nova.

"I'm going to stay and wait for Chloe." Tanner said as he stretched out across the couch.

I slipped my hand into Ryker's and leaned my head on his shoulder as we walked to the front door.

The next day began as most had. I got up, got dressed, got coffee. A flicker behind me caught my attention.

I jumped before I realized who it was. "Jesus, Marcus, can you not blip up out of nowhere directly behind me?!" I placed a hand over my heart and glared at him.

"My apologies, Karah. Are you ready for today?" His tone said he was anything but sorry.

"Today? What's happening today?" I asked as I took a sip of the delicious coffee in my hands.

"Today we begin your intensified training."
He gave me a look that said I had no way out of this.
"Did your father not tell you?"

"Must've slipped his mind." I grumbled as I
brought my coffee cup to my lips again.

"Once you finish here, meet me in the
training room." He pointed, indicating to the cup in
my hands.

I gave him a thumbs up as I took a large drink
from my mug.

After about an hour of mentally preparing
myself, I met Marcus in the training room. As I
walked in, I noticed much of the equipment had
been pushed to the sides of the room and a large fire
extinguisher was just behind where Marcus was
standing with his hands behind his back.

"Should I be worried about that?" I inquired
as I pointed to the extinguisher.

"Do you think you should be?" He didn't even
bother looking at where I had pointed.

"Well, now I do!" I said, a little louder than
was necessary.

"We're going to trigger the abilities you have
already used." He brushed a piece of lint from his
shoulder as if this weren't a monumental moment
for me.

"Ah, fuck." I mumbled to myself.

"To begin, concentrate on the catching fire."
He finally acknowledged the glaring red instrument

in the room with a wave of his hand. "Hence the extinguisher."

I closed my eyes and focused on concentrating. I tried to replicate the anger I had when Adriel kissed me. I attempted to force the rage and hatred I had felt. Nothing. I tried again, thinking about the men who had attacked me. Still nothing. Not even a smolder. I opened my eyes and released a sigh of defeat.

"Try again Karah." Marcus coaxed in a patient tone.

I took a deep breath, closed my eyes, and clenched my fists. This time I thought of UMBRA. The experiments. The pain. The absolute helplessness I felt any time they would come into my cell for another bout of injections and scans. Finally, a small amount of smoke began to rise from my palms.

"YES!" I exclaimed. I saw that Atticus had been standing by the door as he quickly walked away. I shrugged it off. Moments later, he reappeared at the door and took a step in.

"Karah. I have an idea." He was hesitant with his words. Adriel stepped out from behind him.

"Oh, fuck no. Nuh-uh." The smoke disappeared as my concentration was broken.

Marcus stepped forward. "Hold on Karah. He may be on to something." Adriel had stepped past Atticus, further into the training room, and took position in front of me. "Adriel, what did you do to set her off the other day?"

Adriel smiled a devilish smile. "This." He quickly stepped forward and once again kissed me.

"FUCK!" I screamed. I pulled my arm back and extended, connecting with Adrie's cheekbone. He stumbled back. As my fist rushed past my head, I could feel heat coming from it. Both of my hands had once again caught fire. My head jerked towards Marcus, then to the door. Everyone had gathered by there. Ryker's fists were clenched as tightly as mine had been. I think if he could have caught fire at that moment, he would have. Christian was leaned against the doorframe with his arms crossed and looked amused. My father stood front and center of everyone with a proud smile across his face. I watched as Chloe and Tanner gave each other a high-five.

"Now, we have to amplify that." Marcus nodded to Adriel, giving him the go-ahead.

Adriel rushed me, linebacker style. I caught the glimpse of Ryker being held back by Des, Clay, and Christian. I grew angrier as Adriel dropped his shoulder into my stomach. My entire body went hot. The flames engulfed me entirely as I flipped ass overhead and landed in a crouched kneel. Adriel turned and attempted to rush me again from behind. As I turned and stood, I landed an upper cut to the bottom of his jaw. He flew back and landed on the flat of his back. I heard the breath knock out of his chest as he landed. The group at the door erupted into applause.

"Good, Karah." Marcus was watching the event intently. "Let's see if we can concentrate the fire."

"You mean, like shoot it?" I looked down to my hands with excited anticipation.

"Yeah, exactly." He said with an appraising look on his face as he studied me.

"Okay then." I thought for a moment. Newton's first law of motion. An object in motion will stay in motion unless acted upon by an outside force.

With that thought I reared back like I was a pro-league baseball player and cranked my arm as if to through a fast pitch. A blazing sphere hurtled toward Adriel. With a wave of his hand, the ball changed direction and flew headlong back at me.

"Fucking hell!" I screamed as I ducked. Adriel had an all too familiar smug look plastered on his face.

I threw again. And again, he sent the flaming ball back to me. This time I caught it. His smugness disappeared. I threw it again. However, this global inferno was twice the size of the original. Adriel put his arms up to protect his face as the fireball made contact. Marcus promptly grabbed the fire extinguisher and smothered the flames coming from Adriel's sleeves.

"Okay, kids, that's enough for today. I'd rather not have to start a burn unit here." My dad said as he walked over to me. "Uhm, honey, mind putting the flames out there, kid?" he gestured at the flames crackling from my body.

"Yeah, about that. I'd like to but uhm...I'm not really sure how." I started to slightly panic as I took in the flames surrounding me.

"That'd be my cue." Ryker commented with the smallest amount of glee, from the doorway as he hurried to me. The smile on his face was enough comfort to calm me and snuff out the flames. He leaned in and gave me a kiss. "Good job, baby." He added with a wink.

I looked across the room and saw Adriel, brushing the ashes from his arms. It gratified me to see the sullen and irked expression on his face. I knew it was petty to be happy he was annoyed, but I couldn't help it. While he may not have fully lied about my father, I still hated him. Ryker and I made our way to the door and to the rest of the group who immediately began to give me high-fives and pat me on the back. Including Atticus who seemed to enjoy watching his brother get smacked around.

As we all collectively walked out of the training room and my ego was still distended, I made a spontaneous decision. Taking Ryker by the hand, I glanced at him and bit my lower lip.

"We'll see you guys in a little bit." I called out over my shoulder to the group.

"Wait, what? Where are we going?" Ryker was genuinely confused because this is when we usually spent time with our friends.

"You'll see." I gripped his hand a little tighter and smiled at him mischievously.

I lead him to his room and closed the door behind him.

"Why are we in my room?" He asked as he looked down at me. "What are you up to, doll?" His voice was a mix of apprehension and excitement.

"What I'm about to do, my dad REALLY doesn't need to see." I replied as I pushed his solid build against the dresser. My heart raced. I ran my hands up his powerful chest and into his hair and pulled his mouth to mine. He gingerly bit my lower lip. Our tongues crashed together like waves on a beach. He broke our kiss as he leaned down and ever so carefully bit the side of my neck just below my jawbone, quickly kissing it. My hands had slipped from his hair down his body and raised his shirt up past his head and off him revealing his god-like build, with every muscle tightened.

My fingers were nimble as I unfastened his belt and looked into his eyes. There was unfiltered lust and adoration shining back at me through his dilated pupils, I could barely see the beautiful blue of his irises. I dropped to my knees in front of him, looking up at him from where I kneeled.

Expeditiously, I pulled his jeans and boxers from where they rested on his hips to just above his knees. His member was already standing erect as I held his eyes and ran my tongue from the base of him to the ridge of the tip. He sucked in a breath and let out a slight grunt as I circled his tip with my tongue and placed a kiss to the head. As I ran my tongue up and down his shaft, I heard Ryker let out a deep moan. After I adequately teased him, I took the tip of him into my mouth and all the way down to his base. His hand went to my hair as my head bobbed up and down on his thickness. He tried to restrain himself from moving his hips into my mouth until I placed my hands on his thighs and dug my nails in. That was all the permission he needed as his hips started moving back and forth. I hollowed out my cheeks and rolled my tongue over him as he let out another groan, this one louder.

His breathing started to quicken, and his hips became sporadic. "Karah," He was breathless, and I felt a rush go through me knowing I was the one to cause the undoing of this man, "I... can't...I'm going to- "I continued my ministrations and brought him to the back of my throat and swallowed. "Fuck, babe...don't stop." His hips stalled as I kept bobbing my head up and down his shaft. He let out a guttural groan as he released in the back of my throat and I swallowed every drop of his warm saltiness.

"Fuck!" Ryker quietly exclaimed.

Still on my knees, I looked up at him and wiped my bottom lip with my thumb. He leaned and cupped my face, guiding me off my knees until I was face to face with him.

"I love you, Karah. And not just because of your incredible mouth." He kissed me deeply until a crash from the common area lead our attentions astray.

"What the fuck was that?!" I asked, bewildered.

Ryker heaved his pants up and grabbed his shirt as we bolted for the door and down the hall to the common area. As we entered the room, Ryker's pants still undone, the group was laughing as Tanner was attempting to sweep up broken glass.

"What the hell happened?" The annoyance clear in my voice.

"Genius here…" Nova began and pointed at Tanner, "thought he was skilled enough to carry a tray of glasses on his head and dropped all of them."

"What?! I figured if people could carry baskets on their heads, I could carry this!" Tanner replied in his own defense as he stood up.

I paused to take a moment to digest the idiocy that brought my time in the bedroom with

Ryker to a screeching halt. "I fucking hate ALL of you!!" I exclaimed.

Chloe who clearly had read my and Ryker's thoughts, erupted into uncontrollable laughter.

"All of you, I say!!" I half yelled and half chuckled.

Christian, who had finally put the clues together, laughed and said, "Aw man. Sorry guys!"

I could only respond with a dignified middle finger.

∞Six∞

I made it a priority to train daily with Marcus to be able to harness my power and use them when I wanted to. My ability to control people was solid. I could turn it on and off like the flip of a switch. My fire skill was much more difficult to rein in. I had learned to control my emotions and tap into them when I need to, rather than being a slave to my anger and allowing it to control me. While I could keep the flames from dancing across my fingers, I still hadn't learned to keep my eyes from changing. Not that I really minded that all too much. I had even forced myself to be in the same vicinity as Adriel so that I could practice keeping myself in check. I hadn't dared attempt to bring out the creature that killed the men who attacked me in the alley. I had zero control of that monster. However, Uncle Reed was confident he found out why I had blacked out that day. Fear. My fear had overwhelmed me, causing me to disassociate myself from the monster. The fire was triggered by anger, this...thing, was triggered by fear.

Marcus attempted to convince me to agree to release, what Tanner graciously named, the siren. Every time he would bring up the topic, I avoided it or tried to change the subject. I wasn't ready.

After our daily training, Marcus said, "You know we're going to have to tap into that ability sooner or later, don't you Karah?" He tried to be gentle about his approach of the topic.

"I know. I know." My shoulders dropped because I knew I couldn't avoid it any longer. "We'll give it a shot tomorrow. How does that sound?"

"That's fair. I'll make sure to set up precautions." He seemed pleased that I was finally willing to broach the subject.

"Yeah, that would probably be best." I nodded in agreement.

I was hesitant to tell Ryker that I had made plans to wake up the siren. He knew that if anything were to happen to Marcus during training because of this thing inside of me, it would crush me completely. I had become close with most the members of the compound apart from Clay and Adriel. Not that I didn't attempt to get Clay to open up to me. He sure knew how to stick to his guns when it came to keeping people at arm's length. I knew I had to tell Ryker, but he was on a mission with Christian and Desmond and it would have to wait. Luckily, he was set to return that night.

In the meantime, Tanner and I worked diligently with the party planner to create the perfect party for Chloe. Somehow, we managed to score a Dippin Dots cart for her. We had a fantastic DJ booked, and the decorations were everything she would love. Workers set up a stage at the front of the room reserved for parties. My dad even came up with a good idea and had a candy bar set up and made sure the bartenders learned a specialty drink for her. She put up with so much, we wanted her to know how much we loved and appreciated her. One way or another, we were able to keep Chloe from sneaking into the room and spoiling the surprise. Luckily, I only had to keep her from it for one more day.

The day droned on as I waited for Ryker to return to the compound. The darkness of the witching hour had fallen upon the compound and there was still no sign of him. My anxiety began to take over. Immediately, I began to think the worst, that Ryker wasn't going to be coming home. As my body started to shake, the door swung open. Desmond, Christian, and Ryker dragged in. Dirty and bloodied.

"What the hell happened?!" I shouted as I rushed to their sides.

"Ah, don't worry, Karah. We've been through worse." Christian said, wiping the blood from his lip.

I turned to face Ryker and was met with the left half of his face covered in blood.

"Please tell me that's someone else's blood." My voice was pleading.

"Some of it probably is." Des commented as he wiped some smoot from his brow.

"Fucking hell." I said as I retrieved the first-aid kit stashed in the kitchen, hot water, and clean towels. "Sit." I barked pointing to the couch. As I washed the blood from Ryker's face, I could see a long cut down the side of it. It was deep enough that another scar would be added to his already multitudinous collection. Luckily, the cut skipped over his eye. A wound like that would surely have left him blind in that eye.

"You're going to need stitches. You ready?" I asked as I grabbed the sutures from the kit.

"Nah, stitches aren't necessary." He leaned away from me and rested his head on the back of the couch.

"Uh yeah, they kind of are, Tristan, your face is cut open." I had never used his first name before then.

"Ooooo Ryker's in trouble!" Des joked with a chuckle.

"Can it, Desmond!" I snapped. I was in no mood for jokes while the man I loved was bleeding.

"It just needs a couple of staples to keep it closed. Hand me that." Ryker said, pointing at the medical grade stapler.

"Are you crazy?!" He couldn't be serious right now.

"Babe, trust me, it'll be healed by tomorrow, just let me see it." He held his hand out to me expectantly.

I crossed my arms. "No way, let me get it stitched up."

Ryker let out an exasperated sigh and reached past me as he grabbed the stapler. He promptly held the open skin together with his fingers and stapled the open wound.

"That stings a little." He huffed. "See, all better." I could tell he was trying to lighten the mood with a smile.

"Yeah, that's sanitary. At least let me put some antibiotics on it." I grumbled as I reached for the ointment.

"Once you bring those lips over here." He smiled a half-cocked smile and tapped on his own lips. I obliged, leaned in, and gave him a relieved kiss.

There I sat, putting antibiotic ointment down the sloppily closed wound, as I examined it. "As much as I don't like the fact you just stapled your own face..." I paused. "it was kind of hot. But let's refrain next time please? Better yet, just don't get hurt. I kind of want you around for a while."

He laughed, "Kind of?"

"Just a little bit." I laughed, holding my thumb and forefinger together showing a small space.

"Oh yeah?!" He once again laughed and swept me onto his lap.

I adjusted myself and straddled him, my arms wrapped around his neck. I looked into his immaculate eyes. "Yeah." My voice was barely above a whisper, as I leaned in to kiss him again.

From the other side of the couch, a pillow flew, hitting me in the back. "Ya'll get a room!!" Des laughed after heaving the pillow at us.

"Not a bad idea." Ryker said with a playful smile as he squeezed my sides.

"Not tonight, soldier boy. Not while you're hurt." I slyly repeated his word back to him.

"Oh, that's just messed up." He groaned as he dropped his forehead to my chest.

I smiled triumphantly. The sudden realization that I still had to tell him about the upcoming training session slid forefront from the back of my thoughts. "I do have to tell you something though."

"I don't like the sound of that, is everything okay?" He looked up from my chest into my eyes.

"Oh, yeah." I hesitated, worried what he would say. "I just...finally agreed to test out my other ability."

"Oh shit, the siren?!" Des was far too excited for someone who clearly had been eavesdropping. "I gotta see this." He rubbed his hands together like he was ready to dig into a big feast, not witness the horror that is the siren.

Ryker shot him a threatening glare.

"I'll uh, I'll just be going now." Des gave a half-smile as he skittered down the hall.

"Are you sure you want to do that?" Ryker's voice was full of concern.

"Yeah, babe. It's time." I nodded my head and started to play with the hair at the back of his neck.

Hesitantly, Ryker replied. "If you're sure. When is the session?"

I looked at the imaginary watch on my wrist. "In about four hours."

Ryker's face immediately went from shock to mild annoyance. "Bed. Now." He swatted my butt so I would stand.

"Yes, sir." I smiled, stood up, and took his hand so we could both get some much-needed sleep.

The next morning, I woke early. I wanted to surprise Chloe with her birthday gift before my training session with Marcus, so I made my way to her room and opened the door. My eyes widened at the sight on the other side.

"Oh god! Sorry guys!" I laughed. I had managed to walk in on Chloe and Tanner in the throes of early morning birthday sex and Tanner's luminescent white ass. I backed out as quickly as I had walked in. Before closing the door, I remembered the interruption Tanner caused to Ryker and myself. "Isn't karma great?!" I laughed as I shut the door.

My exclamations seemed to wake some of the others. Nova came rushing down the hall.

"Is everything okay?!" She reached for the doorknob.

"I wouldn't." I said with a smile and stopped her hand from turning the knob.

The look of sudden realization crossed her face as she threw her head back and laughed. Nova and I made our way to the kitchen. The news of my impending training session buzzed around the compound.

"You nervous about today?" Nova asked, taking a sip of her tea.

"A little bit." I stared down at the hot coffee I had been holding.

From the opposing hall that led to the lab and my father's office, I heard my dad. "Karah, is that you?" he asked turning the corner.

"Yeah, Dad, what's up?" I questioned in reply and took another gulp of coffee.

"You won't be training today." He told me as he made his way to the coffee pot.

"What? Why? Is this because of the ability?" I was worried that, if I didn't get a handle on it, it could resurface at any given moment. That was not something I was looking forward to ever happening.

"No, it's not that." My dad said as he stirred in a dash of creamer, "Marcus was just called away to take care of something. He wants to resume the session in a few days." My father faced me and started to drink from his cup.

"Oh. Okay. Wait so I got up early for nothing?!" My shoulders sunk and I started cursing the world in my head. I am NOT a fan of waking up early for no reason.

"Pretty much." Dad chuckled.

Christian had walked in with a bit of a limp and sat at the island in exhaustion. Nova immediately began to dote on his every need.

"You doing okay, buddy?" I asked him as I slid him a mug of coffee.

"Yeah. Yeah, I'm just a little sore." He winced as he adjusted himself on the stool. "How's Ryker's face?"

"Perfect as always." I joked. "But I don't know yet, he was asleep when I left the room. I'll go check on him."

I got up from the stool I had been sitting on and walked to Ryker's bedroom. As I entered, Ryker was no longer in the bed asleep. I could hear the water running in the shower. I opened the bathroom door to a room filled with steam. As the dense fog-like mist parted I could see Ryker behind the translucent glass of the shower door. The water streamed down his perfectly toned physique, illuminating every muscle. For the first time, I saw all the scars. Bullet scars, healed over stab wounds, burns. His entire body was covered. But the scars made him that much more beautiful and perfect. I stood silently and welcomed the heavenly sight in front of me. Before my mind could begin to wander, I noticed the staples that had once been in his face, were now in a neat pile on the counter. As I looked back over, I hadn't noticed that Ryker had shut the water off and stepped out of the shower, wrapping a towel around his V-shaped waist. The cut down his face that had been there mere hours ago, was now but a thin pink scar.

"Good morning my love." He said as he stepped up to me and gave me a quick kiss.

My eyes were locked on his new scar. My hand autonomously reached up as my fingers traced it.

"I told you it would be healed." He playfully teased.

"How?" I traced my fingers over the scar again, in awe of the fact the wound was practically healed.

"Dunno," he shrugged his shoulders, "but does it really matter?"

"No. No I guess not. Does it hurt still?" I pulled my hand away because I didn't even consider that it could still be tender.

"Nah, just a little sensitive." He paused, and looked as if he just remembered something, "Wait, shouldn't you be getting ready for training?" His brow furrowed with his confusion.

I couldn't help but become distracted as the tiny water droplets trickled down his body. My hand grew a mind of its own as it reached out and ran down his perfectly sculpted abs.

He snickered, "Earth to Karah." He waved his hand in front of my face to bring my attention back to his words.

"Huh? What?" I said as I snapped back to the present.

He laughed. "Where'd you go there?"

"Straight to the gutter." I smiled. "What were you asking me?"

"Don't you have a very important training session to get to?" The amusement on his face and in his tone was unmistakable.

"Oh! Right. Yeah, no, Marcus rescheduled it."

"Good that means, you're mine until the party, right?" He gave me a sexy smirk as he wrapped his arms around my waist. I could feel his dick as it pressed against me.

I groaned. I wanted nothing more than to rip his towel off and let him bend me over the bathroom counter.

"I can't." I pouted and stuck my bottom lip out for dramatic effect. "I have to oversee the party set up. Apparently, this party planner is too incompetent to do things the way Tanner and I want them."

"It's okay, doll. You go get 'em." He said slightly disappointed but still smiling.

"You really are perfect. You know that, right?" I was clearly pointing out the obvious to a man who was oblivious to his own greatness. I ran my hand down his still stubbled cheek.

"I'm really not. Our broken parts just fit together perfectly." He gave me a sweet smile. "I love you." He nuzzled his nose across mine and kissed the tip.

"I love you too." I replied. With a sharp inhale, I whined, "I gotta go."

"Go." He said and gave my ass a playful smack as I turned to walk out.

The time for Chloe's party drew near. The set up was uneventful seeing as how I only made two of the workers cry. I went to get ready. Digging through the unnecessary amount of clothes in my closet, I settled on the short red satin dress I had bought when I first got to the compound and a pair of black, peep-toe stilettos with black rhinestones that embellished the entire shoe, that I purchased specifically so I wouldn't have the same shoe catastrophe as I did on my birthday. My hair was in loose curls falling down my back. From under my hair, peeked the python tattoo that covered my back. I checked myself in the newly replaced mirror, adjusted my boobs, grabbed the blindfold from the dresser and walked out of the room. I walked to

Chloe's room and knocked on the door, as I had learned from mistakes made earlier that day.

"Come in!" Chloe's lively voice sang back from the other side.

"Hey, birthday girl," I greeted her as I opened the door and found her in front of her vanity mirror, "you ready?"

"Yeeeeesss!" She excitedly squeaked. Her flaming auburn hair was straightened, and her lips were red. Her emerald silk dress glimmered as the light caught the rhinestones that were spread across it.

"Look at you! You look beautiful, Chloe!" I gushed at her as I looked at her from head to toe.

She flipped her hair back over her shoulder, "I know, right?!" We laughed.

"Before we go, one more thing." I mentioned playfully, as I held up the blindfold that was hanging from one finger.

"Kinky." Tanner chimed from the doorway.

"Shut up, Tanner." I chuckled at his comment.

I put the blindfold securely over Chloe's eyes and Tanner and I, each holding an arm, led her to her party. As we opened the door, a poppy alternative/indie song played. As I removed the blindfold, Chloe's face lit up seeing all the things that awaited her. Bright rainbow-colored décor covered the wall and tables to match the candy themed bar at the far right of the room. Moving colored stage lights bounced across the room.

"Is that Dippin Dots?!" She squealed. Her reaction made all the work worth it. Tanner and I high fived as Chloe took off towards the cart. He hustled behind her as he attempted to keep up with her pace.

"She's going to be pinging off the walls." I said out loud to myself as hands wrapped around my waist.

"Mmm, hey baby." I said. As I leaned my head back the smell of musk and leather wafted over me. "Fucking hell!" I spun around coming eye to eye with Adriel.

"Well hello to you too, darling." He had a scathing smile on his face.

"Get fucked." I said over my shoulder as I stormed away.

"Is that an offer?!" he called from behind me.

I huffed over to the bar and order my standard vodka soda and after the encounter with Adriel, a straight shot of tequila was warranted.

Christian and Nova had waked up, "Whoa girl, slow down." Christian sounded almost critical.

I shot him an irritated look as I threw back the shot and slammed the shot glass down. Nova's eyes went big.

"Adriel?" Christian questioned eyeing my, now empty, shot glass.

"Adriel." I retorted as I took a sip of my drink and rolled my eyes.

"Adriel did what?" I heard Ryker's solemn voice from behind me.

"Nothing babe. Don't worry about it." I said as I turned to face him.

Ryker looked at Christian which was met with a shrug. Christian and Nova ordered their drinks and went to find the birthday girl.

"You look absolutely amazing, doll." He leaned in and greeted me with a kiss. His black button-up shirt was tight across his chest and arms. His biceps stretched the fabric of the sleeves to the point that they looked like they would burst with just the right movement.

"Mmm, so do you, soldier boy." I returned his kiss with my own.

A slow, romantic song began to play through the speakers set up in all corners of the room.

"Dance with me." Ryker commanded more than asked.

"Always." I replied as he took my hand and led me to the dance floor.

As we swayed to the music, Ryker's hands were firmly on my lower back, I sang along with the words of the song, and I looked up at him. The way he looked at me, the love and compassion shining back at me, made me lose my words. For that one moment earth stood still and everyone disappeared.

It was just Ryker and me alone on the dance floor. I realized in that moment he was my everything. I would never need anything or anyone else, ever again. I couldn't help but to kiss him. As the song ended and an energetic number began, we left the dance floor hand in hand.

"I'll be right back." Ryker said as he kissed my hand and hurried off toward the bathroom.

Still in a love induced daze, I didn't even care that Adriel had took place next to me.

"You used to look at me the same way." He looked over at me, "Do you remember? You would sing to me the same way you sang to him." The tone in his voice was reminiscent yet still spiteful.

"First off, it's fucking creepy that you were watching us, okay." I ticked off the points on my finger as I stated them. "Secondly, me and Ryker? That's real. Unlike whatever you and I were." I never once looked over at him, instead I watched the guests mingle.

"You say that now. But he's not the man for you." The contempt in his words made my hackles rise.

"Eat a bag of dicks, Adriel. Ryker is more of a man than you'll ever be. You don't compare. Not even close. He is superior to you in EVERY way." I finally turned my head to him and looked him up and down. I wanted to make sure he understood the implication. His face contorted from nonchalant to irate as the comment hit him below the belt as it was meant to.

"We'll see about that." He snarled before he turned to leave. As he walked away, Ryker was returning. Adriel made it a point to shove his shoulder into Ryker as he walked past. Ryker stopped dead in his tracks and the look on his face was menacing.

"Oh shit." I said out loud as I rushed over. They stood there, both men's bodies were tensed. They stared at each other like two wolves fighting for the role of alpha. "Ryker come on. He's not worth the time or energy." I commanded, pulling him by the arm. Ryker began to follow my lead.

"Yes. Do as your bitch says little dog." Adriel smirked vilely through his words.

"Ah fuck." I said as I felt Ryker spin, his arm ripped away from my hand and connected with Adriel's face with a loud thud.

Adriel flew back into a nearby table with a deafening crash. Ryker's already muscular frame became rigid. Adriel rushed at Ryker, knocking him to the ground, he continued to punch Ryker hard in the head. The sensation of heat tingled through my body as the flames erupted from both hands. I drew back to throw a flaming ball at Adriel when someone grabbed my arm. It was Clay.

"Let them solve this. It's been a long time coming." There was a general calmness in his voice that I felt was not suitable to the situation.

The guests had formed a crowd as we were talking. Ryker grabbed Adriel and flipped him on his back, his shirt tore and frayed across his shoulders. The two continued to exchange blows until Ryker kicked Adriel in the gut with an extreme force. Adriel slid across the floor slamming into the bar. I looked at Clay, my eyes pleaded for him to allow me to intervene. With a quick nod from Clay, I ran in front of Ryker.

"Babe. That's enough." His rageful expression softened as I approached him with my hands raised.

Ryker walked past me to Adriel and knelt where Adriel was coughing and had been attempting to get off the floor. Ryker grabbed him by the lapels and lifted him from the ground, Adriel's feet dangled like a ragdoll. "Don't ever call her a bitch again." He said through gritted teeth, dropping Adriel back to the ground.

As he walked back to me, he put his arm around my shoulders. "Come on." He guided me out of the room.

We walked back to the kitchen beside the common area.

"Sit down, tough guy." I pointed to the stool. He promptly sat. I grabbed a towel, wet it, and began to clean the blood from his lip and under his nose.

"Sorry." He grumbled.

"It's not me you're going to have to apologize to." I said in a chiding manner.

His face turned to utter shock. "I'm not apologizing to that slimy piece of shit!"

I shook my head. "Not him! To Chloe. It WAS her birthday party after all."

"Ah man." He said disappointed in himself for behaving like that at her party.

"I'm starting to think we should stop throwing parties around here." I laughed.

∞Seven∞

Since the time of my escape, UMBRA had laid low. They were quiet and barely operational, at least, that's what they led us to believe. In the recent months, they had begun to kick up activity. They started to abduct more and more children, took soldiers from the battlefields. They were determined to let no one escape their facilities again. The dead bodies of the failed experiments and found escapees began to pop up across the country. The rise in the brotherhood's activity meant two things. One, Ryker and the other members of the compound were sent on more and more missions. And two, I had to step up my game when it came to my powers. My father would not allow me to go out with the team until I had them fully under my control. After Marcus rescheduled my sessions the day of Chloe's birthday, it had been three days and Marcus finally, was able to get back to the compound for training.

"Ok, Karah. You ready?" Marcus asked. He was equipped in a Kevlar vest lined with magnesium alloy that Uncle Reed built for this session since the siren seemed to have a thing for hearts.

"Yeah. Let's do this." I swung my arms at my sides to loosen up.

"Good. Now concentrate on the creature on the video." Marcus ordered me.

I inhaled deeply to steady myself and closed my eyes. I tried to clear my mind of everything except the creature. But the thought of Ryker being out in danger fighting the brotherhood without me, crept in. I opened my eyes with a heavy sigh.

"Try again, Karah." He demanded.

"I am trying, Marcus! Do you have any idea how hard it is to concentrate on nothing?!" I was already beginning to lose my composure.

"Well try harder!" I could tell Marcus was getting just as frustrated as I was. "Now, try again. Let your fear for Ryker's safety in. Just DO NOT let it take over." His voice was loud, but not in a domineering way. He was just trying to get me to understand the gravity of the situation.

I took my stance, planted my feet, and closed my eyes. Inhaled. I once again thought of the monster, her black eyes, and sharp claw-like fingers. Her shriek. Every time I thought of that sound, I could feel shivers all the way to my bones. The thoughts of Ryker lurched in again. Instead of trying to push them out, I welcomed them. The fear began to set in. All the while I had the image of the siren in the forefront of my mind. My breathing changed, on the verge of hyperventilation. My eyes rolled into the back of my head and my feet raised off the ground. I looked down at my hands. My fingers had been replaced by the black claws I saw in the security footage.

"Karah? Karah are you in there?" Marcus's voice had a hint of a tremble.

There was an exhilarating aroma from his vicinity. Like all the greatest smells one after another, repeating. I glided until I was inches from his face, I could see that he had begun to sweat. I cocked my head, studying him as the aroma seeped into my nose again. I couldn't tell what that delicious smell was, but it was faint and coming from my mentor. I looked past him at the full wall of mirrors he stood in front of. The creature staring back at me was floating approximately two feet from the ground with gaunt, hollow black eyes, and skin as pale as freshly fallen snow. My lips had turned as black as my eyes and my cheeks all but disappeared. I reached up to touch my own face and the reflection mimicked my movements. The claws that had replaced my fingers left cuts where I had touched my skin as if they were made of razorblades. In the reflection of the mirror, Ryker and the rest of the compound residents stood in the doorway. The delicious aroma now came from the group. Strong and intoxicating. At a blistering speed, I flew to the group.

"My god, that smell." I thought. "What IS that?!"

"Karah. Come back to us." Marcus whispered from his place behind me.

Before I knew what was happening, I flew rapidly towards him. I came close enough to him that I could see the siren's reflection in his eyes. I let out the soul piercing shriek I had only heard once before on the tape. I crossed back to the group. The smell was stronger there and I had to find out what it was.

"We're losing her guys." Marcus said as quietly as he could as though not to spook a wild animal. The group began to back up from the doorway and the smell became stronger. Ryker stayed in place.

"Karah. Come back to me, doll." There wasn't even the slightest hint of fear in his voice.

I got closer. He didn't have the smell. Instead, he smelled of sandalwood and fresh rain. I leaned in and inhaled his scent.

"Karah. Come back." He repeated his sentiment and never once broke eye contact.

I could feel my body lower as my feet touched down on the ground. My eyes rolled back once again. As I opened them, I let out a heavy breath, panting. My knees buckled and I fell into Ryker's arm. My face stung from the razor-like cuts. I looked up at him, then to the group. Finally, I turned to face Marcus who was stripping off the vest. I rushed to the mirror to see my own reflection looking back at me. Blood trickled from my cheek and as I reached up and touched the cuts, I realized they were very much real. My father emerged from within the group with a proud smile on his face.

"Good job, Karah. You did great." He said as he clapped both hands on my shoulders.

"So, does this mean I can start going out on missions?" I smiled, hopeful that he would finally give me a chance to prove myself.

"Nice try. You were able to change once and we almost lost you in there." He did not seem amused by my efforts.

All I could do was roll my eyes like a teenager.

Ryker walked me to the couch and sat me down to rest. He then went to the kitchen and retrieved food and water. "Here. Eat. You need your strength."

I gladly accepted the sandwich as the group gathered on the couch. Adriel stayed as far from Ryker and I as possible.

"Man, I really wouldn't want to be on the receiving end of all...that." Des said, motioning at the entirety of my body.

"Yeah, Karah, you're kind of terrifying." Tanner chimed in, still visibly shaken.

"You were ALL scared?" I asked. I was genuinely curious if there was a correlation of their fear and that delicious smell.

The group, for once, all agreed. Except Ryker. He stayed silent, watching me.

"I knew you wouldn't have done anything to me. I had no reason to be scared." He mentioned with a certain casualty, as he wiped a crumb from my face.

"Hmm." I looked down at my lunch.

119

"What?" Christian questioned me. He clearly could tell the wheels in my head were turning.

"I- I think I could smell your fear. All of you had this...aroma. All but you." I looked at Ryker as I took another bite. I'm sure at that point I looked like a chipmunk and was very hard to take seriously.

Clay's phone broke the silence that had befallen the room. He walked toward the hallway before he answered. Moments later there was a deep indistinguishable scream from within the hall.

"Oh no." Chloe's voice, had gone from high-pitched and excited to hardly audible. Her face had gone pale and a look of dread spread across it.

"What, Chloe? What is it?" Tanner asked as he gently rubbed her back.

She barely moved as she looked up. "It was his daughter."

My head snapped from her to the direction of the corridor. Des got up and headed toward the hall. I sprinted over the table and caught him.

"Let me go talk to him." I said as I grabbed his arm. I was aware that Clay wanted to keep people at a distance, but he knew I would always be willing to help.

I found Clay in his room, sitting on the side of his bed. His normal look of constant irritation was replaced by tears streaming down his face.

"Clay?" I asked cautiously, taking only the smallest possible steps into the room.

"Go away." He whispered.

"Clay, we know it was your daughter." He looked up at me. I paused before continuing, "Clay, what'd she say?"

"They have Vanessa. UMBRA has my girl." He dropped his heads into his hands.

I could see a mix of emotions had come over him. Pain, sadness, rage all collid ng together in a never-ending cycle that you could see play across his face. I would rather have seen his grumpy expression over the heartbreaking scene in front of me.

"Then let's go get your girl." I kept my voice quiet. I knew if the others heard, they would immediately put a stop to it.

We agreed to meet at the doors of the compound after everyone else had gone to bed in hopes to keep our plan a secret. We were determined to rescue his daughter by all means necessary, including going in with no backup.

Clay spent the evening triangulating where the call from his daughter came from. My stomach was in knots. I was a giant ball of anxiety, adrenaline, and a touch of guilt. I knew I would have to lie to Ryker, but after all, it was for the greater good. At least that's what I kept telling myself. Later that night after the dinner that I just pushed around my plate, I told him I wasn't feeling well and wanted to go to bed early so I would sleep in my own room. My room, that as of recently, was pretty much a glorified closet since I had slept in Ryker's room almost nightly. I waited until after Ryker came and kissed me goodnight to change into my all-black ensemble. Once the lights went out, I crept to the door and out into the darkness. Clay was already waiting by his car holding a large duffel bag. As we climbed in, running footsteps approached.

"Seriously Karah?" It was Chloe who had been running up behind us. "Telepathic, remember?" She tapped the side of her head.

"Shut up and get in." I whispered and looked around to make sure no one else was with her.

Chloe clamored into the backseat and we took off into the night.

Two hours later we arrived about a mile from the UMBRA facility that has holding Vanessa captive.

"We walk from here." Clay's voice was a low, gruff whisper filled with determination.

As we approached closer to our destination, my heart began to race. The last time I had seen one of the brotherhood's facilities I was running from it, not towards it. Clay stopped running and ducked down. We could see the lights from the small building glowing from behind the hill we used for cover.

"Chloe, how many can you hear inside?" he said as he rifled through the duffel. He began to pull out pistols and multiple magazines. Finally, he slung a sawed-off shotgun onto his back.

Chloe closed her eyes and was silent. "Couple dozen at least."

"Okay, we'll go through the front, find Vanessa, get out. Got it?" he looked at both of us in turn to ensure we understood his plan.

"Wait, all these facilities are built the same, right? And if Vanessa was able to get to a phone, they definitely would've put her in a solitary confinement cell on the left side of the building." I said as I gestured toward the corresponding side. "In the back of the building, there's a cargo bay. That's where they bring supplies and new test subjects in through. It's not far from the solitary cells." I looked at Clay.

"She's right, Clay. That would be the fastest way to your daughter." Chloe agreed, nodding her head.

"Then lead the way." I could feel that he had finally put his trust in me.

Like stealthy jungle cats, we crept through the darkness towards the back of the building.

Once in range Chloe was able to read exactly how many guards were outside.

"There's three. Two by the door and one over there." She pointed toward the far side of the building.

"I'll take care of the straggler over there." Clay began to edge to the other side of the facility. "Whatever happens, you get Vanessa and get out of here. If we get split up, you get her and get the hell out of dodge. Do you understand me?"

"I guess we got these two bozos" I nodded toward the guards in front of us. "We'll get her, you just worry about keeping us clear."

We parted ways. Chloe and I snuck down behind a truck that was clearly beyond any kind of repair. We were three yards from our targets and my eyes went violet. I blew the purple cloud I had grown so fond of, and it covered both guards.

"Nighty night time, douchebags." I concentrated on putting them both into a coma. They fell like a sack of bricks. We spun as we heard rustling footsteps coming from beside us. Clay had rejoined us, blood on his hands.

"Let's go." Clay said, his eyes locked on the door as we ran to it; Chloe grabbed the entry badge off one of the guards and swiped it through the reader. We heard the click of the door unlocking and she yanked it open. As we rushed down the nightmare inducing corridor, flashes of my previous life flickered in my head. Clay ran ahead silently dropping any guards we encountered. We reached the wing that contained the solitary confinement cells. The guard was asleep at the desk. I blew across my hand again.

"I think a heart attack will do nicely for you, tubby." His eyes sprung open as he grabbed his arm and collapsed. I stretched over his lifeless body and pushed the button on the wall, unlocking the set of secured doors. Now we just had to find which cell she was held in. Chloe took one side of the hall and I searched the other, as Clay stood watch.

"Clay!" I whispered, "what does she look like?"

"She's thirteen, brown hair, blue eyes." I felt bad that he couldn't really tell what his own daughter looked like anymore.

I stopped searching for the slightest moment. "Could you be any more vague?! I need something specific!"

I could see him racking his brain. "A birthmark. She has a birthmark on her left forearm."

I peered into window after window. "Empty. Empty. Empty. Bingo." I concentrated my pyrokinesis into one hand, grabbed the lock, melting the metal, and snatched it free.

"Vanessa?" I said quietly so I wouldn't frighten her. Her head had been resting on her knees and her arms covered her face. She peered over her arms at the sound of her name. "Vanessa, I'm with your dad, we have to go. Now!" I stretched my hand out to her. The frail child leapt from the bed and grabbed ahold of me. She was surprisingly strong for such a small girl.

"Clay, Chloe, I got her. Let's move!" The volume of my voice had returned to its normal register.

We took off back through the doors and down the long hall, jumping over the bodies Clay dropped on our way in. I'm confident Vanessa's feet barely touched the floor because of the speed in which I was dragging her behind me. As we sprinted out of the cargo door, the cool night air was crisp and refreshing. The memory of my own escape came back to me as I took a deep breath of fresh air and held it in my lungs for a moment. Clay grabbed Vanessa, wrapping her in a big hug much like my own father had the day I arrived at the compound. Understandably, both Clay and Vanessa began to cry.

"Guys, this is great and all, yay family reunions" I quickly did a silly dance, "but we still have to get out of here!"

We all took off running as fast as our legs would carry us. Clay carrying Vanessa as we ran through the inky blackness. Shots began to ring out behind us as we ran closer to the car. They released the dogs, and I could pick up the sound of them barking and their paws running heavy against the ground. We could see the car. The shots got closer and I could hear as bullets whizzed past me. When suddenly, a blinding pain ripped through my shoulder blade, I fell by the rear tire. Chloe grabbed me and stuffed me into the backseat as the vehicle jerked into motion, speeding down the darkened road.

"Clay, she's been hit, you need to hurry." Her once sweet voice changed to very serious and filled with urgency. She pushed me over and ripped the hole in my shirt where the bullet had entered so she could get a better view of the wound. She stripped off the outermost shirt she was wearing and held it to my shoulder. It felt like an eternity before we reached the compound, and Chloe and Clay scrambled to get Vanessa and I inside. As we approached the common area, we could see the dim glow of the lights coming from the room.

"Fuck." I whispered as I looked at Chloe. In that moment, I knew we were busted.

As we reached the common area, Ryker, Dad, Christian, Nova, Des, Tanner, and Uncle Reed were sitting on the couch. When they saw Chloe practically carrying me and keeping pressure on my back, they bolted over to us.

Ryker had fear plastered across his face. As he reached closer to us, in attempts to relieve Chloe from her position, I let out a nervous, half conscious chuckle. "Hey honey, I'm home." Then I felt myself falling as everything went black.

∞Eight∞

When I woke, I was laid on my stomach on a steel table in the lab. The vociferation of people around me combined with the loss of blood made my head spin. I tried to sit up on my elbows but the faint feeling in my head and the stinging pain in my shoulder wouldn't allow it.

"Karah!" Ryker yelled as he rushed to my side. "Karah, what the hell were you thinking?! You could've gotten yourself killed!" He had never raised his voice to ME before. I can say, I wasn't a fan of it.

"Eh." I said, weakly. "It's just a flesh wound...right?" in my best efforts to lighten the mood.

"We have no idea the damage inside this wound. The bullet is still in there and I'm going to have to go in after it." Uncle Reed said as he walked up with a vial and an unreasonably long needle attached to a syringe. "Problem is, you'll have to be awake because I only have a local anesthetic. This may sting a bit but try to lay still." He looked at the mountainous men who had gathered in the lab and nodded to me. Atticus held one arm, Christian the other. Clay and Des were at the end of the table each holding a leg. Ryker grabbed Reed's rolling stool and sat in front of me to keep his face eye level with mine. "Okay, here we go." Uncle Reed said as he took a deep breath and stuck the needle repeatedly into the injured area.

"That wasn't so bad." I breathed.

"That's not the bad part." Christian leaned down and whispered.

"Wha-?!" I said befuddled as a searing pain radiated throughout my shoulder. What began as a low groan expeditiously turned into a spine-chilling scream that could make even the toughest man wince.

Ryker kissed my head. "You're going to be okay. I've got you." His voice began to shake, I couldn't tell if it was from anger or from him wishing he could take the pain away.

As suddenly as the blistering pain began, it started to dissolve, and I heard the satisfying clink of the bullet hitting the pan resting behind my head.

"Fuuuuuuck!" I managed to get out past gritted teeth. My eyes locked on Uncle Reed who had stepped out from behind me. "You, sir, are a thundercunt. Don't EVER do that again."

"Don't ever get shot again and I won't have to." He smiled, but he meant every word.

"Touché." I said as my field of vision began to blur.

"Uh, Reed?" Atticus's usual cheer in his voice was replaced with worry. "This bleeding isn't slowing down."

"Dammit!" Reed exclaimed as he rushed back behind me with bandages and began to pack the wound.

I could only make out the shape of something small as it came ever closer. "Am I in heaven? Is that an angel?" I thought, "No, too small to be an angel. Maybe it's an imp and I'm in hell."

"Vanessa, you shouldn't be in here." Clay commented to his daughter from his position at the foot of the table.

"Oh, yeah, the kid. That makes more sense." I concluded the thoughts within my own head.

Without a word, Vanessa gently nudged Uncle Reed from where he stood, holding pressure on my shoulder.

"Vanessa?!" Clay's voice sounded similar to my fathers when he became stern with me.

She replaced Uncle Reed's hands with her own and I could hear her take a deep breath in through her nose and slowly exhaled through her mouth. As she did, a warmth radiated from the hole in my shoulder. It was soothing, like drinking hot tea with honey when you're sick. Slowly, my vision restored, and the room was silent.

"What just happened back there?" I said over my shoulder, trying to see, and completely confused.

"Uhm...I- I think she just HEALED your shoulder!" Tanner exclaimed in utter and unabridged shock. He had been standing behind Uncle Reed out of the way of the commotion.

"What?! Let me see! I gotta see this, someone get me a mirror!" I said, excitedly, with my hand open. Seconds later Ryker put the requested mirror in it. I adjusted to see my shoulder in its reflection. "Well, ain't that just the cat's tits?!" Where there once was a bloodied pit was now a round pink scar. I looked at Ryker. "Look baby, we match!" I laughed half-heartedly but he was not amused, his solemn expression dᵢdn't even flicker.

Atticus and Christian helped me as I sat up, making sure I didn't lose my balance. I was face to face with Vanessa and could finally see the girl in more than just the dim bulbs of the facility. She was frail. Her brown hair was matted, and her face was thin. Looking at her, I saw a lot of myself when I was held by the brotherhood. Her blue eyes were dim and lifeless, and she had freckles that dotted across her face.

"Thanks kid." I stretched my arm in a circle, flexing my shoulder. I smiled at her, essentially letting her know she did a job well done.

She replied with only a faint smile before she silently turned around and walked from the lab, with Clay at her heels.

"How is it feeling?" Uncle Reed asked as he poked, pressed, and fiddled with the new scar.

"It's a little tender. My shoulder itself is kind of sore. But considering everything, not too damn shabby." I stretched my shoulder again.

"Good. Good." He snapped off his latex gloves, threw them in the pile of used medical equipment and collectively tossed it all in the metal trashcan.

"Everyone out please. I think Ryker and I need to have a conversation with the kamikaze, here." My father said from where he stood at the edge of the lab with his arms crossed across his chest.

Des put his hand on my arm as he walked by. "Good luck, friend-o."

My father might as well have had the word *Disappointed* scrawled across his forehead.

"Dad, I can explain." I started. "She was alive, I know the facility's layout, it just made sense."

"No!" He yelled, cutting me off. His arms left his chest as he began to wave them to emphasize his point. "What would have made sense is coming to me. I would have worked up a SOLID plan and sent in a team who could have handled it!"

"But Dad! I DID handle it! I got her out." I tried my best to come to my own defense. "She's alive because we went and got her!"

"You didn't handle it! You got shot! You could have died because you're too damn stubborn to wait! And she's alive because you got lucky." His face had turned an interesting dark shade of burgundy which was my way of knowing he wasn't just mad, he was livid. He grew silent for a moment before he looked from me to Ryker, "I'll be in my office. Ryker make sure she gets to bed and STAYS there." He gave me one more disappointed glare before he left with a huff.

Ryker raised his head out of his hands and looked at me. I couldn't make eye contact with him. I kept my gaze down on my blood-stained shoes. I knew he was pissed at me too. That thought hurt me more than my father being angry with me.

He finally spoke. "You lied to me." His voice was much softer than his expression had been.

"I know Ryker and I'm sorry. But I had to." I still couldn't bring myself to make eye contact with him.

He scoffed. "No. No you didn't."

"You wouldn't have let me go if I had told you the truth." I said quietly, wanting to disappear from that moment.

"No, I wouldn't have let you go without me. I know better than trying to tell your stubborn ass not to do something." He knew that I was like a child in that aspect. Tell me not to do something, chances are I'm going to do it. "I would have gone and made

133

sure you made it home WITHOUT an extra hole in your body."

I finally forced myself to look at him. Before I could say another word, Ryker swiftly sprung from his seat in front me. His hands firmly holding my face. He bent his head down with a powerful kiss. I could feel every emotion pouring out of him and into me as our lips danced. Anger, relief, lust, love all wrapped into one raw passionate moment. He rested his forehead on mine. I panted; his kiss left me breathless.

"Don't ever pull this shit on me again. Okay?" his eyes locked onto mine as though he was trying to see if I registered what he had said.

"Yes, sir." I let a small smile slip across my mouth. "Wait. How did you guys know we left?" I asked, the thought hadn't come up until now.

"Tanner." He gave a slight shrug.

"Fucking Chloe." I said more to myself than to Ryker.

"Now, let's get you to bed. In MY bed." He carefully helped me off the table, to his room, and into his warm bed.

The sun rose too early that morning. I had only fallen asleep a few hours before the light of day crept across the room. Ryker was already awake when my eyes fluttered open. His finger was delicately tracing the new scar on my shoulder. I laid on his chest motionless, I enjoyed his every touch. He tried to slide out from under me without disruption and out of the bed. My grip on him tightened ever so slightly.

"Not yet." I mumbled while exhaustion refused to leave me.

"I'll be right back. I promise." He said as he left the bed. He delicately kissed my cheek and moved the hair from my face before leaving the room.

I grabbed his pillow, curling it under my face. As I did, I took a deep breath in, breathing in his scent. His fragrance meant home to me. It indicated safety, security, and everything I r ever had before. My comfort was disrupted by the feeling of eyes being on me.

"Babe, didn't we talk about you staring at me? It's still creepy." A hand rested on my arm, with no words. "Ryker?" I peeked through my hair that had fallen back down over my face. Instead of Ryker sitting next me, it was Adriel. "Ugh, what do you want?"

"I just wanted to make sure you were okay, darling. I heard about last night. You always were a headstrong one." He voice was a soft, almost concerned, tone.

"Please just go away, Adriel." I laid my face back onto Ryker's pillow.

With a light tap of his hand on my arm, he rose. "As you wish." He quickly walked away.

"Am I still asleep or was that ridiculously easy?" I thought to myself as I snuggled closer into lump of fluffy comfort.

"Why was HE in here?" I heard Ryker's voice from the door as he looked down the hall in the direction Adriel had walked.

I rolled over to face him. "He was checking on me. But hey, he left when I told him to, so small miracles."

"Good." He grumbled. I could tell he was in no mood to deal with any of Adriel's shenanigans.

"Is that coffee, I smell?? I asked as I lifted my head up.

"It is. Here." He offered me one of the cups he was holding. "Extra shot of espresso."

"You're a god among men." I sat up, seized the cup, and took a large gulp.

He chuckled and sat on the edge of the bed. "I have nothing planned for today. What do you want to do?" He asked as he put his hand on my leg.

"You're not going to let me out of your sight, are you?" I asked as if I didn't already know the answer.

"Not for a while, no." He shook his head.

"I don't know, babe. I guess we can just hang out here." I really didn't have the energy to do anything.

"Still tired, huh?" he said with a slight smile.

"Mmhmm." I nodded and took another sip of coffee.

"That's a shame." His smile grew wider and he winked.

It took a moment for my still half-asleep brain to connect the dots on what he said. "Oh, you dirty bird!" I leaned up and quickly kissed him.

He chuckled lightly at my comment. "Let's get you some breakfast."

I hadn't realized how hungry I was until that moment.

When we entered the kitchen, Clay was sitting with Vanessa. He was studying her face while she ate her cereal as if she would disappear again. He glanced up from her and smiled at me. That was the first time I had ever seen him smile.

"How ya doing, Vanessa?" I asked and sat across from her, setting my coffee cup down in front of me.

Her eyes darted up from where she had been staring down into her bowl.

"She still hasn't said anything." Clay whispered to me. "She only points." I could tell he was concerned but I think he was just happy that they were reunited.

"She just needs time." I looked from Clay to Vanessa. "Right V?" I gave her a knowing wink.

She smiled her small smile as Chloe and Tanner walked in, hand in hand.

I glared at Chloe for a moment. "Big mouth."

"What?!" she exclaimed with a mix of surprise and confusion.

"You told Tanner? Really?" I pointed to him. "We all know he can't keep his big trap shut!".

Chloe looked at Tanner as if she was asking for back up.

"She's right, you know." He said as he took a bite of the banana he had grabbed from the counter.

"I just wanted someone to know where we were, in case something went wrong." Defensively, she threw her hands up.

"Yeah, I told Christian an hour after you guys left." He shrugged and Chloe smacked him in the stomach.

"Seriously, Tanner?! You're supposed to be backing me up here!" she squealed.

"What?! Have you seen her?!" He pointed to me. "She's scary when she's mad!" He exclaimed with a mouth full of banana.

This exchange seemed to have caused Vanessa to giggle. The sound that came from his daughter made Clay light up like a child on Christmas morning.

"Thank you." He mouthed, without letting a sound escape his mouth.

"You're welcome." I mouthed back. Despite the fact that I took a bullet to the shoulder and pissed off the two men most important to me, I was proud of myself.

Dad entered the kitchen n a seemingly much better mood than he was the night before.

"Why don't we all take the day?" he clapped his hands together. "There's been a lot of excitement. Let's welcome our new resident properly, shall we?" he motioned to Vanessa.

"NO PARTIES!" Tanner, Chloe, and I all exclaimed in unison as all our heads snapped to my father.

This caused everyone in the kitchen to erupt into laughter. All except Vanessa of course, considering she had no idea what we meant by it.

"No parties." Dad agreed with a smile. "How about a movie night instead? Pizza, junk food, movie marathon? What do you guys think?"

"Sounds good to me." I shrugged.

"Samsies!" Chloe said excitedly. Any excuse to have candy and junk food meant she was automatically in.

"Then it's settled." I could tell he was pleased.

Ryker and I volunteered to go get the snacks and movie night accoutrement. More like I

139

volunteered and a slightly more protective Ryker, got dragged along for the ride. We drove down the road, hands intertwined. As we shopped for all the snacks requested by our housemates, a woman walked past us. She was a blonde woman, slightly taller than me and had to be in her 40's. I watched as her eyes roamed over Ryker, taking in every delicious curve of muscle. I put my hand in his back pocket, in a way to say, "This is mine." I heard her scoff from behind us. I smiled to myself, pleased with my moment of pettiness.

Ryker chortled. "I saw that." He said as he cut his eyes to me.

"Oh? Whatever could you be referring to?" I choked out as I attempted to keep a straight face.

"I fucking love you." He leaned and kissed my head and began to laugh.

As we turned down the aisle, the woman had started to come up from the opposite end. She glared at me with intent in her eyes. She reached where we stood, looking for the multiple candies Chloe had requested.

"Excuse me." she said as I tilted my head toward her. "Yes, you. I'm sorry but I don't think your behavior in a public place is appropriate." She directed her unsolicited comment towards me. I looked behind me to make sure no one was standing behind me just to be sure it was, in fact, me she was speaking to.

"Okay, lady." I tried my hardest to let the comment go.

"You should have a little more respect for yourself and others." Her snide remark was steadily increasing my annoyance.

"Get fucked." I said as I went back to looking for Chloe's snacks and made my best attempt to ignore this woman completely.

"You're rude and shouldn't be grabbing a grown man's butt in public. It's inappropriate and there are children here."

"Listen here you dried up twat-waffle, no one asked for your fucking opinion." My temper started to show. "Quit being a jealous hag and get over yourself."

The woman, with her face in shock, looked at Ryker. "You could do so much better than HER." She said as she looked me up and down.

Ryker seemed to take more offense to this comment than I did. He grabbed me, immediately drawing me into a passionate French kiss. My middle finger rose high and proud right in the bitchy woman's face, never breaking the kiss. He pulled away from me and finally addressed her, "No...no I really couldn't." With that he popped my butt with just enough force for it to sting.

The woman looked appalled and hurried away from us which caused Ryker and I burst into laughter.

"And you talk about me!" I laughed, placing my hand in his back pocket once more.

Once we made it back to the compound, we shared our adventure at the store with the group.

"We can't let you two go anywhere without causing a scene, can we?!" Christian bellowed with laughter, holding his sides.

"Perhaps we should get them collars and keep them on leashes!" Atticus roared. The innocence in his voice was clear that he did not mean the comment as many of us had taken it.

"Kinky!" Tanner responded to Atticus. To which most of everyone could only shake their heads and roll their eyes.

Ryker and I locked eyes and smiled. It was clear we both had the same lewd thoughts at the idea of a collar.

∞Nine∞

We all gathered in the theater room of the compound to watch the movie, including Adriel's perpetually angry self. The room had dark burgundy curtains that covered the walls and the same shade carpet. Unlike in actual movie theaters, the chairs were loveseats that reclined fully. There were eight, in total, all spaced accordingly to allow room to be stretched out. There were small tables situated next to each of the seats and a large screen bolted to the wall at the front of the room. A shelf next to the door held multiple blankets and pillows to allow for ultimate comfort.

Ryker and I walked hand in hand as we found our seat at the back of the room. I had never been in the theater room before since I had spent most of my free time training or breaking up fights between Ryker and Adriel.

"Hmm…Well, at least the carpets match the drapes." I mentioned, aloud, laughing at my own joke along with scattered laughs from the members of the group who had already come in.

"Dork!" Christian called out from his seat with Nova, toward the front of the room.

Finally, the flick began to stream across the large screen, some action movie I didn't truly care about. One by one, the loveseats began to recline. The couples snuggled in closer to one another. Ryker and I got comfortable and stretched out the recliner.

Fingers intertwined; I laid my head on his shoulder. Thirty minutes went by. Ryker looked over to where I had laid my head on him and, instinctively, I looked up at him. He leaned over and began to give me a kiss. It started as a quick, light peck on the lips. But something took us over and the kiss slowed and became deeper, our tongues danced together. He shifted his weight to his side to face me, he let go of my hand and grabbed my hip. As he fiddled with the elastic band of my shorts, I rolled from my side to my back, giving him permission. His hand dipped down the front of the soft cotton shorts. Gently, he started to run his fingers over my lips in a teasing, tantalizing motion. I gasped at the sensation of the feather-light touches and he began to massage my clit. Slow, purposeful circles that had just the right amount of pressure to have me writhing in my seat. As the wetness began to build, I covered my mouth as I let out a soft moan. Ryker softly bit my shoulder before he kissed the spot. "Look at me, Doll." His voice was barely a whisper and it was hard for me to hear him over the beating of my heart and the pleasure rushing through my veins. I forced myself to look in those beautiful, blue pools and his trademark smirk graced his face.

His fingers glided down and teased my opening. As he slid two fingers inside of me, I gasped at the sensation and tried to close my eyes and let my head fall forward, but he nudged my chin with his nose and ran it along my cheek until he was speaking in my ear. "Give me your eyes, Doll. I want your eyes. I want to see the look on your face as I fuck your sweet pussy with my fingers. I want you to see and know exactly who is doing this to you. To see who will be doing this to you for the rest of our lives." He softly bit my neck and ran his tongue over the spot, and I let out another soft moan. My body tightened around him as he pumped them in and out of me. I grabbed his arm as I could feel myself nearing the finish line because of the look in his eyes and the words he spoke to me. His thumb simultaneously rubbing my bundle of nerves. His fingers continued to probe, to curl, to find the spot inside of me that caused me to see stars as my breathing picked up and I had to bite my lip to keep my moans in. The combination of internal and external incitement caused me to peak, gripping his sleeve tightly. I uncovered my mouth, breathing heavily. He caught my mouth with his and devoured the breaths that were panting from my body. "Cum for me, baby. I want to feel you clench around my fingers and your juices cover them." He leaned back and watched my face intently. I. Was. Gone.

My insides gripped his fingers and my thighs locked up around his hand. I looked into his eyes as I found my release and felt wave after wave crash over me. I started to come down from my high and all I could see was Ryker. He gave me a look full of lust as he removed his hand from my shorts and placed his fingers in his mouth, sucking them dry. He closed his eyes and let out a small grunt as he tasted me on his fingers. I swear I could've cum again just from watching him taste me. When he took every drop of me from his skin, he looked back at me and smirked.

"You good?" he leaned in closely and whispered, biting his lower lip. His breath sent a tingle throughout my body and there was an unmistakable excitement in his voice.

"I'll let you know when the blood returns to my brain." I whispered back still trying to catch my breath and slow my heart from beating completely out of my chest.

I scanned the room to make sure no one had viewed more than the movie that was playing and to ensure the blanket muffled the sounds that escaped me. To my relief, no one had seen what had just occurred. Except one set of eyes and they raged with a seething hatred. Adriel had watched the entire event unfold as if it were the movie on the screen.

As the movie ended, many of the group were asleep. Adriel was the first out of the door. Ryker, Chloe, Atticus, Christian, and I were the only others awake. While Christian carried Nova to bed, Ryker and Atticus sat on the couch and discussed the movie, meanwhile Chloe and I went to the kitchen to get drinks for us.

She looked at me, knowingly and lightly shook her head. "Dirty!" she said in a hushed tone and looked behind us making sure no one could hear what we were talking about. "Dirty, dirty girl!"

"Is nothing private with you?!" I pulled her further away from the group that remained in the common area, looking to see if anyone had heard her.

"Oh please. If you wanted it to be private, you probably shouldn't have screamed so loudly in your head! It makes it kind of hard to block out!" she said with an evil smile. Well, as evil as she could possibly produce.

"My bad." I chortled. "But to be fair he has amazing hands." I returned her devilish grin.

"Oh, dear lord, I didn't need to know that!" she said much louder than she had been speaking. Her voice immediately quieted down again. "But like, amazing amazing or AMAZING amazing?"

"AMAZING amazing." We laughed together at our inside conversation as we returned to the couch with the drinks. As Christian returned, Ryker excused himself.

"Be right back, nature calls."

I rolled my eyes playfully.

"Hey Atti, your brother seems to have a bit of a staring problem." I said as I sat back and got comfortable and took a sip of my drink.

"I wonder why." Chloe snorted under her breath which received a quick elbow jab to the side. "Ah! My spleen!" she cried out. Which caused all of us to laugh.

"Yes. Well, he tends to become...fixated." Atticus replied casually.

"You don't say." I mumbled under my breath.

Ryker returned to the couch. "What are we talking about?"

"Adriel's staring issues." Christian yawned through his words.

Ryker looked at me. "Tell ya later." I leaned over and told him quietly. I certainly couldn't tell him exactly what Adriel had been watching at that current moment.

Sleepily, Nova stumbled into the common area. One pant leg was to her knee, the other dragged under her foot. Her shirt was half falling off her shoulder. Her blonde hair that was once in a neat bun was hanging loosely off the top of her head.

"Hey there sunshine." I chuckled as I directed my attention to the still half-asleep Nova by the doorway.

She pointed to Christian. "You, bedroom. Bring the tortilla chips, cheese dip, and a Dr. Pepper with you!" Then she proceeded to stagger back down the hallway.

"Coming dear!" Christian immediately got up from his seat on the couch.

"If it were anyone else, and I mean ANYONE else, I would question that." I laughed as Christian gathered all the things Nova requested.

"See you guys in the morning." Christian smiled and gave an attempted wave with his hands full.

"They probably have the weirdest foreplay ever." I said unintentionally out loud rather than in my head. Ryker choked on his drink, Chloe inhaled part of a chip and started to cough, and Atticus laughed his booming laugh.

The night was drawing late as the remaining members of the group drug in slowly through the compound and into their rooms. Clay carried Vanessa to her bed and Tanner looked reminiscent of a zombie as he teetered down the hallway.

"I'm going to go to bed too." Chloe began to skip away and attempted to catch up to Tanner. Presumably to make sure he didn't crash into a wall.

"Goodnight." Ryker and I both said. I began to pick up and take the dishes and bottles into the kitchen.

He started taking a few of the empty bottles to the trashcan. "You coming to bed, babe?"

"Yeah, I'm just going to get all this cleaned up." I motioned with full hands to the mess we seemed to have created out of thin air.

"Okay, I'm going to take a shower. Don't be too long." He gave me a playful wink.

"Wouldn't dream of it." I quickly raised my eyebrows at the thought of him in the shower.

He kissed my cheek and walked off to the bedroom. Moments later, Adriel entered the common area.

"You make a mess, you clean it. I'm almost done here." I told him, without even looking in his direction.

He stepped closer to me. "Do you do these things just to get under my skin?" He asked, his voice was cold and angry.

I began to wash the remainder of the dishes. "I don't even think about you, Adriel. If what I do gets under your skin, that's just a bonus."

He stepped up behind me. I could feel his breath on the back of my neck. "You do think of me, don't you? Of us? How I made you feel?" He ran one icy finger down the side of my throat.

The flashbacks of mine and Adriel's year together flickered across my mind. Bursts of the nights we had spent with one another blinked across my thoughts.

"He will never be able to make you feel the way I can. The way I have." He whispered as he leaned closer to my ear.

Slowly, I turned to face him. His hands were on either side of me and gripped the sink. His lips were inches from mine. My eyes traveled from his chest up to his face.

"You're right Adriel. He will NEVER make me feel like you did." My voice was quiet as I looked him in the eye.

The look of victory spread across his cold, pale face.

"He will never make me feel like a worthless piece of trash. He will never make me feel like I'm unloved or unwanted. He will never make me feel like I was only ever good for a fuck." My eyes never broke contact with his. I had much more confidence in my words than I had before.

The victorious look that has been on his face quickly faded and was replaced by anger as his hand clenched tightly around my throat cutting off all air.

"You'll see. One day you'll see that you're worth is what I tell you it is." He hissed in my ear.

With a quick knee to the family jewels, he released his grip from my throat and grabbed where my knee hit him. My hand instinctually went up to my throat. "Touch me again and I'll kill you myself." I promised rather than threatened.

The next day, Marcus arrived at the compound for our training session. "I heard you went on your own mission." He said as we walked to the training room.

"Yeeeeeeaaah." I assumed he would've been upset with me for going out before he and my father authorized it.

"How was your control?" he asked with what was almost a hint of pride in his voice.

"It was great. I didn't have any trouble." I told him as I sat on the floor and stretched out my muscles.

"So, then how'd you get shot in the back?" Any glimmer of pride that had been in his voice disappeared.

"A, it was the shoulder and B, it was completely non-power related." I tried desperately to redeem myself in the eyes of my mentor.

"Which means, you've been slacking on your physical training." He paused and waved Atticus in the door. "Atticus will be your sparring partner today."

My eyes grew large and my jaw dropped. "You can't be serious! That's like trying to fight a pissed off T-rex with proportionally lengthed prosthetic arms!"

Atticus chuckled at the thought of himself as a dinosaur.

"Even a T-rex has its weaknesses. Now begin." Marcus said with a curt nod.

Atticus and I stood opposite of each other and he let out a terrifying roar as he charged at me. Apparently, he was taking the t-rex comment seriously.

"Fuck!" I screamed and leapt out of the way and tried to kick him. He grabbed my leg, spun me, and released. I sailed into the wall of mirrors. I bounced as I hit the ground, shattered glass rained down around me. I groaned, my less than graceful landing knocked the wind out of my chest.

"Again." Marcus's tone was calm.

Atticus charged again, I slid between his legs and kicked backwards, hitting him square in the rear. It was like kicking a metal drum full of concrete and the shockwave caused me to lose balance and land directly on my hip.

"Again!" Marcus yelled this time. "Watch for his weaknesses."

"Like what?! I'm fighting a damn dump truck!" I yelled back. I knew I couldn't use my abilities to get out of this one.

Atticus rushed for the third time. I turned and ran, with enough frictional force, I was able to run up the wall, backflip, landing on Atticus's shoulders. I immediately wrapped my legs tightly around his neck and flung myself backwards using momentum to my benefit. We both flipped and landed with a loud crash that shook the room.

"Good Karah! Now we're going to make this a bit more difficult." He smiled a very uncharacteristically sly smile. "While your opponent has their weaknesses, so do you."

"Harder?!" I was in disbelief. Was he mad enough to try and get me killed during training? "What kind of crack have you been smoking?!"

Nova joined us and attempted to help Atticus off the floor.

"You never know what kind of power or biological weapon you will encounter. Some powers allow the host to change into another person. Like Nova for example." He motioned to her. She changed into Chloe, back to herself, then into Christian.

"Yeah, I stick by my foreplay comment now." I thought out loud as she morphed from person to person.

"What?" the imposter Christian asked, quizzically.

"Oh nothing." I smiled and laughed off the comment I made the night before.

"We're going to work on your weakness." As Marcus said that Nova turned into Ryker. "Your weakness is Ryker. You fear for his safety constantly. If you can't get past that, you will NEVER be able to go on a mission with him. Now begin."

My brain knew it wasn't really Ryker, but my eyes weren't convinced that it wasn't him.

"No. Absolutely not. I can't do this." I shook my head. There was no way I could hurt even a fake Ryker.

"You can and you will." He waved to Nova, indicating for her to start her assault.

I could feel my eyes grow hot. But not because of any powers. The tears that my eyes began to produce, stung them.

The Ryker clone rushed me. I couldn't move. All I could do was stand there and stare. He slammed into me like I got hit by a charging rhino. I slammed back into the wall with a cry and fell to the floor on my hands and knees.

"Again!" Marcus yelled. I stood from the floor and let my arms land limply at my sides as I got back into position.

He blitzed a second time. I still couldn't bring myself to hit him. Once more, I got knocked to my ass.

"Again!!" Marcus yelled louder. Every time I failed his voice would get a decibel louder.

Another attack with the same result. I was flat on my back.

"Karah, you have to fight! Now, AGAIN!!"

As the Ryker double rushed for the fourth time, I looked at Marcus. "I don't have to do shit." I flew backward again.

Marcus's face changed from annoyed to pleased. "Good job Karah." His voice was softer this time.

"Wait, what?" I groaned as I propped myself up against the wall and rubbed where my head had connected with the floor.

"Your weakness isn't Ryker. Ryker is your strength. You'll do anything to make sure he doesn't get hurt. And he would do the same for you." Marcus smiled a triumphant smile.

"It could be the possible concussion Nova just gave me, but I'm confused." I winced as I rubbed the spot on my head again. "Ow."

"Your weakness is, you're easily tricked and manipulated." He put his hands behind his back and rocked back and forth on his feet. "I was testing to see if you would be manipulated by me, to hit who you thought was someone you cared for."

Nova walked over to help me up and extended her arm.

"Low blow, dude." I brushed myself off and reached up to take Nova's hand.

"But it's true." Nova shrugged. "Sorry hon."

"Thanks...traitor." I gave Nova a look of annoyance and acceptance. After all, it WAS true. I mean, I DID spend a year with Adriel. I finally was fully back on my feet when my father entered the training room.

"I think that's enough for today. If she hits the wall like that again, there will be a Karah shaped hole in it." He pointed to the wall I had recently become well acquainted with.

"Who do I look like to you? The damn Kool-Aid man?!" I asked as I picked parts of chipped cinderblock from my shirt.

"Come on, I want to show you something."
He waved as a beckon for me to follow him.

I limped my way out of the training room
behind my father to his office.

"Here, sit down." He pulled out his plush
leather office chair, offering me the seat.

"Ahhhhhh." I sighed in relieve. It was like
sitting on a cloud, and my sore body was thankful for
the cushion.

My father retrieved a large envelope from the
center drawer in his desk and put it in front of me.

"What's this?" I asked as I looked up at him
with my face in a full state of confusion.

"Open it." He said quietly and nodded to the
dull yellow envelope.

I slid the contents from its packaging. The top
page read *Employee file #051664.* Clipped to the
corner was a photo. I recognized the woman in the
photo from somewhere when it hit me.

"Dad...is this...." I trailed off, unable to finish
my own sentence.

"Yeah, kiddo, it is." He put a reaffirming hand
on my shoulder.

I flipped the page to the employee
information. *Name: Anna Decker. Position: Lead
Biological Researcher.*

"Dad, what company is this for?" A sudden
chill ran down my spine and my stomach turned. I

knew the words that were coming next, but I was hoping I was wrong. Please let me be wrong.

"It's an UMBRA file. Clay grabbed it when you guys went and got Vanessa." He pointed to the UMBRA letterhead in the corner that I had so clearly missed.

"She's an UMBRA employee..." I was trying to wrap my mind around this information, but it just wouldn't sink in. "She's a RESEARCHER for the brotherhood?" I dropped the stack back to the desk.

"Yes, it appears so." He let out a heavy sigh.

I pushed the file from me, and it slipped from the front of the desk, the papers lightly floated to the floor.

"Of course, she is." I said through grit teeth. I got up from the desk as I reached the doorway to the office, I took off running. I went straight to Ryker's room and slammed the door. I began to pace. My mother did this. I thought she just handed me over because of the hatred she felt for my father, but this was all for her own selfishness. When Ryker finally found me in the room, I was seated on the floor, my back rested against the wall, holding my knees in complete darkness.

"Karah? Are you in here?" He flipped on the light. "Whew, thought you took off on me again." He said with a joking smile until he saw my body language. "What's wrong doll?" he asked and immediately rushed to my side and put his arm across my shoulders.

Without raising my head "She's been working for the brotherhood the entire time." My voice was muffled by my face being against my knees.

"Who, Karah?" he asked and rubbed my arm where his hand had been resting.

I met his gaze. "My mom."

∞Ten∞

It had been a week since I found out the truth about my mother. About whom she really was. I stayed in Ryker's room and had not come out as I pieced the puzzle together. My mother's betrayal festered inside of me like a disease. A disease I had to kill off. Every time I thought about the woman who gave birth to me, my blood boiled. I would go from a full emotional breakdown to wanting revenge in the matter of seconds. I spent many nights of that week in tears. Ryker stayed by my side the entire time, silent and stoic when I needed it. Other times he would hold me and whisper reassurances in my ear.

I always thought I hated Adriel. This made me truly understand the meaning of the word hate. However, I couldn't allow myself to stay haunted by her. It was time for me to try and get past this.

The sun had already gone down by the time I decided to emerge from the bedroom. If it hadn't been for Ryker's encouragements, I probably wouldn't have. As I slowly made my way down the hall toward the common area, I could hear the group chatting amongst themselves. As I came into sight, all talking ceased.

"Don't stop on my account." I gave them a tired smile as I walked over to where Ryker had his hand held out for me, grabbing it as I settled beside him.

"How are you doing?" My dad asked. I knew Ryker had been keeping him apprised of the emotional turmoil that had been taking place behind the closed door of the bedroom.

"I'm going to be okay." I gave Ryker's hand a gentle squeeze.

"Good. Do you need anything?" My father's concerned voice made my chest squeeze.

"Just to get back to training." My focus changed when I noticed a few missing faces. "Wait, where's Clay and Vanessa?"

"Oh, uhm, he asked me to give you this." Desmond reached in his back pocket and pulled out a small, folded envelope. "They left the compound."

"Oh! Uhm, yeah. Okay, I guess that makes sense." I said as I tucked the letter into my back pocket. I knew whatever it said would cause me to cry again. He got his daughter back and while it would never bring his wife back, he had a chance to start over.

"Do you want anything to eat?" Chloe asked softly.

"No. Thanks. Just some water." I plopped, exhausted, on the open seat on the couch.

"Coming up." She gave me a sweet smile.

"When can I start training again?" I asked my dad.

"You sure you want to get back in there?"

"Absolutely." That was one thing I was completely sure of.

"I'll call Marcus in the morning." My dad responded.

"Thanks, Dad. Where's Uncle Reed? Don't tell me he left too." I didn't like the idea of losing so many members of my mismatched group. I couldn't handle that on top of everything else.

"No, Reed is giving a seminar this weekend at Brown." Dad eased my trouble mind.

"Oh okay, cool." Chloe brought me a glass of water. "Thanks Chloe."

I sat there, quietly, as the group resumed their chatter. Slowly, I got up and started to walk back to the bedroom without a word. Ryker caught up with me.

He cut in front of me and stopped me. "You okay, babe?"

"Yeah, I'm just going to go to bed. I'm tired." I rubbed the dark circles that had formed under my eyes.

"Okay, I'll be right there." I don't think he trusted when I said I was going to go to bed before him. Especially since the last time I did, I ended up with a bullet in my shoulder.

I made my way to the bedroom, changed into one of Ryker's tee-shirts and crawled into bed. I leaned off the side of the bed and grabbed the letter from Clay out of the back pocket of my pants.

Dear Karah,

I'm sorry to be writing you like this. I've never been good at goodbyes. I suck at them really. I feel like I never really gave you the chance to get to know who I really am as a person, and I'm sorry for that too. I've decided to take Vanessa out of New York. I bought a plot of land out in the middle of bum-fuck nowhere, Wyoming. It would take me a lifetime to thank you for everything you have done for me and Vanessa. She finally spoke. She wanted me to let you know she will always be your little sister, whether you like it or not. She reminds me a bit of you. Like a smaller, less-fowl mouthed, you. I will always be grateful for you and what you've done. I will forever be in your debt. I will write to you as soon as we get settled. Don't kill Adriel. And hold on to Ryker for as long you can. No matter what happens, you'll always be welcome here. You are part of our family and always will be.

With all our love,
Clay and Vanessa.

I was right about his letter because seconds after I finished it, out came the waterworks. I looked up from the paper to Ryker standing in the doorway watching me read.

"What'd he say?" He nodded toward the letter in my hand.

163

I handed him the letter. "He got my name right for once!" I laughed through my tears.

"Awe babe." He sat on the bed and hugged me. "They'll be fine. You did good, doll."

He stood up and began to strip as I wiped my tears. I had forgotten how truly beautiful he was. I became lost in thought. Clay's letter gave me some much-needed clarity. I had a family now. I had my dad. I had Ryker, whom I loved unconditionally. I had the group. I could even learn to tolerate Adriel. But I had a family, without HER.

"You okay, doll?" His question was full of curiosity.

"You know what...yeah." I nodded slowly as I met his gaze. "Yeah, I'm okay. I'm perfect really." I smiled, a real smile, for the first time in a week.

"There's the smile I missed." He said as he climbed into the bed.

"Come here so I can give you something else you missed." My smile widened.

"Ooooo!" He laughed.

I wrapped my arms around him and pulled him close. "I missed you, soldier boy." With that we shared a kiss only seen in the movies. I rolled over, Ryker laid behind me and wrapped himself around me.

"Hey big spoon?" I said quietly over my shoulder.

He lightly laughed, "Yes little spoon?"

"I love you."

"I love you, too." He reaffirmed and kissed the scar on my shoulder.

The next day, I met Marcus early in the training room. I was determined to get my physical training and power training to the best of my ability. I spent four hours training. With my new-found determination, I learned to cage the rage and release the siren without losing control of her. My assumption about the aroma I had kept detecting was accurate. I could smell fear when I released the siren. Since the group was had seen me unleash her so many times, they were no longer scared of her. I sparred more with Nova since I learned that whoever she turned into; she had their powers as well. Granted her abilities in their form weren't as strong as the original person she copied was, it was oddly therapeutic to fight against myself and the siren. We spent most of the day training even through lunch until Marcus made us call it for the day.

"You're getting stronger, Karan." I think I had finally, thoroughly impressed Nova since I came to the compound. We walked towards our rooms.

"Thank god for small miracles, right?" I laughed as I walked into Ryker's room.

He was laying on the bed, watching tv. Shirtless and wearing my favorite grey sweatpants.

"Hey babe, how was training?" He looked from the tv to me.

"It was great. I'm going to ask Dad if I can start going on SANCTIONED missions now."

"He's at a late business meeting now. Some weapons manufacturer wants to become part of Clark Enterprises." He stretched, causing his muscles to flex.

"I didn't know Dad even worked with weapons manufacturers." I said as I began to strip my sweaty clothes off.

"That's because he doesn't. But they wouldn't stop until he met with them."

"I'll just ask him when he gets home. I'm going to get a shower."

"Okay babe." I could feel his eyes roam over my body as he watched me walk to the bathroom.

I got out from under the steaming water, swaddled myself in a towel, and stepped in front of the mirror, wiping the condensation from the glass. As I wiped, Ryker had walked up behind me. He wrapped his arms around my waist and rested his chin on my shoulder.

"Good shower?" he asked.

"Yeah. I feel better." I stared at his eyes in the reflection of the mirror.

"Good. What do you want for dinner?"

I turned in his arms to face him. "I'm not hungry." I ran my hands over his scarred chest.

I looked up at him and dropped the towel to my feet. He looked down at my wet naked body and bit his lower lip. He knew it drove me nuts when he did that. As if he knew exactly what I had in mind, he grabbed me by the hips and hoisted me up as I wrapped my legs around his waist. Carefully but quickly, he walked to the bed, and threw me down on it. I gave a quick bounce off the mattress as I stared up at him and I slid myself back resting on my elbows, with one knee pulled up, my other leg hanging off the side of the bed. My heart raced as he slipped off his grey sweatpants that I loved so much. He took his last step to me, my breathing quickened. He leaned and kissed the inside of my knee. I could see the hunger in his eyes as he drew nearer. My lips met his halfway in a greedy kiss, he grabbed the back of my head pushing me harder into it. He laid me back as our legs became entwined. He bent his head down and softly nibbled my neck and he kissed a trail starting between my exposed breasts and down to my stomach. He bit down harder on my hip and I felt a surge of pleasure burst through me. As he made his way back to my lips, he pushed my knee down and used his own to spread my legs. I could feel his hard length press against me as he kissed a line up my neck. "I want to taste you. My tongue on your sweet cunt as you ride my face with abandon. I want to lick

167

up every drop as you cum for me before I take you with my cock and watch you lose all of your senses beneath me." He pulled back and looked into my eyes. "Is that a good idea, Doll?" He had that mischievous smirk on his face, and he looked at me with so much desire in his eyes.

I couldn't speak, which was a first for me, so I bit my lip and gave a slight nod of my head. He let out a growl as he brought his lips to mine again before quickly kissing a second trail down my body until he reached the apex of my thighs. With my legs spread so wide apart he had a completely unobstructed view of my most private of parts. He looked at my center and licked his lips, "Beautiful," he murmured before his head dipped and he gave a long lick all the way up my lips to just below my clit. My head fell back against the bed and I tangled my hands in his hair as he gave me another deliberate lick.

"So fucking sweet," another lick. "God, Doll, you taste like heaven wrapped in gold." He circled my opening with his tongue before he plunged it inside of me. I let out a cry as my body writhed beneath his onslaught. His tongue left me to return a split second later to my clit, and I felt a finger slide inside of me. I managed to pick up my head and look down at him, and it was one of the most erotic things I had ever experienced.

"Ryker..." I breathed his name and his eyes found mine. I could see the edges of his grin as he picked up the speed with his tongue and finger. His pumps were timed perfectly with the strokes of his tongue. I held his eyes as the familiar pressure began to build inside of me. I ground my hips down into his face as I lost all control as my release blazed a trail through me, and I cried out.

He removed his finger from me and rose from between my legs. His chin was slick with my juices and his features were nothing but pleased. He wiped his chin with the back of his hand before he slowly crawled over my body until he was positioned at my core, the head of his cock rubbing my opening sending another thrill of arousal through my body. "Are you ready for me, Doll?" His voice was low and husky with his desire.

"Yes, please." I was begging and breathless and I am not ashamed to admit it. A l l I wanted was to feel this man fill me and to take him to the clouds with my body like he did for me.

He placed his elbows on either side of my head as he snaked his hands into my hair and held me in place, keeping his eyes on mine. I wrapped my arms under his as he supported himself on either side of me. I could still feel the tip of his hardened manhood teasing my entrance. As the head of his cock entered me a mix of a gasp and moan escaped my lips. He sunk himself all the way into me and let out a deep breath at the feeling of finally being joined in the most intimate of ways. "Karah," he grunted, "you're so fucking tight." He pulled himself almost all the way out and thrust back into me, harder this time. "You feel amazing wrapped around my dick." He started a steady rhythm after that, and I could already feel myself racing to the edge again.

"Ryker!" I cried out as he leaned up and grabbed my hips, raising them slightly to get a better angle. "Oh god, yes, right there. Fuck." I looked down to where we were connected as I saw him pumping in and out of me. My eyes flew back to his and I saw so much love and passion in his eyes that I fell even more in love with him in that moment.

He began to thrust faster. My nails scraped down his back which made him bury himself deeper into me. His hand gently wrapped around my throat under my jaw applying only the slightest amount of pressure so I would keep my eyes on his. "That's right, baby. Give me those eyes. I want to watch you come unglued." His jaw clenched and he let his head drop back for the briefest of moments as he let out a groan from the back of his throat. His head came back up and his eyes locked onto mine again as he started thrusting harder. Our bodies were in perfect rhythm with one another. I could feel my body quiver around him as he moved in repetitive motion. I moaned loudly, without a single care about anything except this moment. I flexed my muscles around him. A moan left his perfect lips as my hips moved, meeting his.

"Cum for me, doll." He whispered. "I can't last much longer. You feel too fucking good." He gritted through clenched teeth. His words sent a ripple through my body. I let out a quiet scream as I did what I was told. My muscles clenched around him as stars burst behind my eyes and I screamed his name. The pleasure he granted me caused his own release, his hips became random and the grunts leaving him sounding almost animalistic and he thrust once, twice, three more times and sank all the way into me as his cock pulsed his hot seed into me.

He collapsed next to me, both of us covered in sweat. He looked at me, his hair obstructing my view of him. I reached over and moved the hair from his face to see his eyes.

Our eyes met. "I love you so much, Tristan Ryker."

"I love you more."

"Unlikely." I sighed with a smile and closed my eyes as I enjoyed our moment of ecstasy.

After about an hour of recovery and another quick shower, Ryker and I went to the common area. Dinner had completely slipped our minds.

"Why are you both wet?" Tanner asked cluelessly.

"It's called a shower there, bud." I smiled as I replied.

"Oh...OH!" he exclaimed as the sudden realization of what I said struck him.

Chloe and I looked at each other and laughed. Chloe gave me one of her looks as to ask how it went. I knew she was listening so in my head I told her, "It was perfect. He is perfect." She smiled back at me.

"Oh shit, I almost forgot! Where's Dad? I have to ask him about going on missions."

Christian checked his watch. "Hmm, no clue. He should've been back by now. He probably went for drinks after dinner."

I sighed. "Dammit, I really need to talk to him."

"Me too. We need to talk about a mission he and I were discussing the other day." Ryker added.

I bumped him with my hip, playfully. He proceeded to whip a towel and popped me on the butt.

"Oh, it's ON!" I yelled and grabbed the sprayer from the sink and sprayed him with the cold water. He began to chase me, and I began to run. Naturally, because my complete lack of grace, I slipped on the water I had sprayed and landed flat on my ass with a loud thud. An eruption of laughter followed.

We all ate dinner together, talked, joked, and laughed. That night, the entire compound was in perfect harmony. Surprisingly, we all got along with Adriel as well.

The next morning, I woke up startled as someone banged on the bedroom door.

"The fuck?!" I cried out as the sound of the banging made me jump.

"This had better be good." Ryker grumbled as he threw the door open.

Christian had been the culprit that had woke us. His face was a mix of fear and concern.

"Uh, bud. What's going on?" as I clumsily climbed out of the bed and crossed the room to the door.

"It's, uh, It-. Here, just read this. It was pinned to the front door." He handed me a folded note. I had never seen Christian speechless, so I knew it couldn't have been anything good.

I opened the note:

Karah,

If you ever want to see your father again, you will meet me where your journey began. Don't make me wait. The consequences will be detrimental.

Anna Decker

"FUCKING BITCH! I WILL END HER!" I screamed. Ryker grabbed the note from my hand.

"Oh shit."

"Who is Anna Decker, Karah?" Christian asked completely confused.

Apparently, my father hadn't told them about her. "The pestilent cunt who pushed me out of her toxic twat." I said as I grabbed my phone to call Uncle Reed and Marcus. Christian's jaw dropped. "Get everyone up, NOW." I ordered as I dialed Marcus's number.

I called Marcus and Reed and explained the note, who Anna Decker was and to meet us at the compound. Everyone had woken up and staggered into the common room where I showed them the note. Once again, I explained who Anna was and that she worked for UMBRA.

"We're getting my dad back. One way or another." I knew it was risky going after Anna, but I had to get my father back home where he belonged.

Adriel slowly approached my side. "Karah, I might be out of line here, but you may want to calm down and think of a plan of attack."

"You're right, you ARE out of line and don't tell me to calm down!" I snapped. I could see the reflection of red from the window behind him. I took a deep breath and closed my eyes and opened them as I released the breath. "Sorry, you're probably right."

We all gathered in the conference room to create a plan.

"What does she mean by "where your journey began"?" Nova questioned as though she was trying to piece the puzzle together.

"It has to be the facility I was housed at." I shrugged, allowing my arms to slap against my legs. "That's where they did the experiments, and I got my powers. It's where I found out who my father was. That's where this all started for me."

"I thought we took care of that facility. Didn't we burn it to the ground?" Christian asked, trying to rack his brain to remember.

"Well, either way, that's where we're going." I could still remember the building and the area around it like I had escaped yesterday.

Everyone suited up in their black military styled uniforms that were worn when they went on missions. Each of their names were on the shoulders. I walked into my dad's room next to his office and sat on his bed. Tears began to roll down my cheeks. I knew he hadn't been in my life long, but he was my father and I loved him dearly. On his dresser, laid a neatly folded uniform. As I picked it up, I could see my name printed on the outer shoulder of the sleeve. I hugged it close to my chest.

"We'll get him back babe, I promise." Ryker found me hugging the uniform in my father's bedroom, I'm sure it was a pitiful sight. He pulled me to his chest and held me.

We drove for what felt like an aeon. A caravan of large black SUV's. I said nothing, just looked out the window and watched the trees pass by. Memories of my past life at the facility flashed between the trees. The foliage disappeared as we approached a massive clearing with the charred remains of the facility. I could see a group of around a dozen militarized men who all stood in a perfect line. We stopped the cars and climbed out. As we made our descent down the field, I could see a man on his knees. His hands were bound and there was a black bag over his head. As we advanced closer a man walked toward us.

"Welcome Karah." A man, who I assumed oversaw this particular event, took a few steps towards us.

"Where the fuck is she?" I growled.

"Oh, you mean, Ms. Decker? She's not here. She just wanted to see if you'd actually risk your life to save his. By all means," He stepped aside and gestured to the bound man with a sweep of his arm. I could recognize my father's nice business suit was torn and his platinum watch now had a large crack across the face. "Take him."

The guard standing behind the man on his knees, ripped the bag away from his head to reveal my father, bloodied and bruised. As though they decided instantly and cohesively; Adriel, Ryker, Christian, Des, Tanner and Atticus all rushed toward the men and my father like a stampede. The sound of the soldier's weapons rang through the air. Adriel instantly threw his hands up causing an invisible telekinetic wall. That's when I heard Nova's shriek, reminiscent of the siren's.

"CHRISTIAN!!!!" her voice was filled with the most gut-wrenching anguish I had ever heard.

∞Eleven∞

I turned to see why Nova had screamed. As I followed her terrified gaze, the world began to move in slow motion. Christian's body went limp and fell to the grass. Nova and I both raced to his side. Nova scooped up his head, laying it on her lap. Another heartbreaking scream left her mouth as she cried, cradling Christian. Suddenly, life snapped back into full speed movements.

"Marcus! Blip them back to the lab, now!" I screamed. I could feel the tears as they began to rise, and I forced them back. He grabbed Nova's shoulder, in a blink, they were gone.

"I want all of you to back up right now! I'm ending this. Right here. Right now." I told the remaining members of the group as I strode to the front of our group.

"You can't do this by yourself, Karah. Please, don't try to do this alone!" Ryker gave his best attempt to get me to reconsider.

"I'm doing this." I met his gaze and I saw fear in his eyes. Fear for me. "I love you, but you can't stop me and I'm not going to let you get hurt in the process." I realized I was pointing to where Christian fell.

The group began to retreat at my order. Ryker never left my side and Adriel never once let the wall falter. He reached were I stood, and the wall held strong. I closed my eyes. I knew what I had to do. In an instant, I began to rise from the ground. My eyes went from brilliant red to inky black, my hands became the claws I remembered from the training session. Except this time, they were on fire as well. My entire body lit ablaze as I floated above the ground. A guttural, spine-tingling scream rose from inside me and was freed from my mouth as I dropped my head back. One I had never heard before. Not like Nova's or the siren's. I heard the gasps of my intended targets. Many of the men began to flee, leaving only 6 of their comrades.

"Drop the wall, Adriel." My voice was ominous and pitched low with the sirens influence.

"NO! Are you insane?! You're not going to die today." His voice was a mix of defiance and pleading.

My head snapped to look at him. "If you ever truly loved me, drop the fucking wall."

He hesitated as he considered his next move, and he dropped his hands.

"ADRIEL!" Ryker screamed. "PUT IT BACK UP!" Adriel took a few steps backward.

Like a Lockheed SR-71 Blackbird, I tore across the field, obliterating the men who stood opposite me. In a matter of moments, some men's throats were ripped from their necks. Two of their heads laid a few feet from their bodies, while others were charred piles of flesh. I left the man who first addressed us when we entered the field, for last. He brandished a pistol and fired at me, hitting me with almost every shot. I never stopped advancing. My morphed body began to push the bullets back through the wounds in which they entered. I was mere inches from the man as my claw-like fingers curled under his chin and wrapped around his face.

"I know she can hear me through that earpiece." My voice was low and bone-chilling. "I'm coming for you Anna." I addressed her through the piece in the man's ear and focused my eyes back on his. "I hope she can see this too, because I'm going to show you your heart." My clawed hand shoved into his chest, the bones protecting his heart broke and splintered. I pulled my hand out, revealing the still pulsating organ to the man it had previously belonged to. As his body fell to the grass, I dropped the heart next to him.

I lowered to the ground behind my father and I returned to my true self. Blood dripped from my body. I looked vaguely like something resembling *Carrie* after the prom. One clawed finger remained as I cut the binds holding my father. Despite being covered in multiple people's blood he hugged me.

"I knew you could do it. Now, let's go. Christian needs us." He knew as well as I did, Christian was our main priority now.

We drove as fast as the bulky vehicles would take us. My dad hung up from the phone call he made as we entered the cars.

"Ryker, I thought about that mission. I think it should be a go." Dad looked back from the front seat to Ryker.

"Yes sir." He nodded.

"Now, Ryker." My father sounded stern but not angry.

"Now?!" Ryker's voice was shocked.

"Now." There was a sense of confidence in his words.

"Yes sir." Ryker replied with a small smile.

All the while, I had barely listened to the conversation they held. I was concentrating mainly with wondering how Christian was doing.

"Karah?" Ryker asked as he took my blood covered hand. I had tried my best to wipe the blood off onto my pants before getting in the car, but they were stained.

"Huh? Yeah?" I turned my attention to him rather than my thoughts.

The smile that was on his face faded. "You okay, doll?"

"I will be. We just need to get to Christian."

"I just got off the phone with Nova. Christian is in surgery. They'll call me when he's out." My dad reassured me.

"Good." My eyes met Ryker's.

"Marry me." He said without any kind of hesitation.

"Wha- what?!" I had thought I misheard him.

"Marry me, Karah. I have a ring, but I didn't expect to do this here or now."

"YOU wanna marry ME?" I gestured to the blood-soaked uniform I was wearing.

"Something a little less…bloody, would work too." His glorious smile reemerged on his face.

I looked to my father. He had the same smile he had when he planned my birthday party plastered to his face and he gave me an approving wink.

"So? Will you, Karah Clark, do me the greatest honor and marry me?"

"Of course, I will, Ryker!" I squealed. As I leaned to kiss him, Ryker immediately stopped me to wipe blood from my face before completing the kiss.

While irrevocably and unconditionally happy, Christian's well-being was still on the forefront of my mind. A surgeon employed by my father had already been waiting at the lab. Luckily, Uncle Reed had the forethought to have him come and set up just in case. Uncle Reed lived by the motto of "Better safe, than sorry." As the convoy screeched up to the front of the compound, my feet had hit the ground before the car had come to a complete stop. I ran through the compound to the lab. As I entered, I saw that the back of the lab had been converted into a makeshift operating room. I could see Christian laying in medical bed that had been wheeled in and Nova met me at the door.

"Is he-?" I whispered, tears once again welling in my eyes.

"No, he's alive, but in bad shape." Nova's cheeks were tear-stained, and her eyes were pink.

"Is he awake?" I tried to keep my voice low in case he was resting.

"Yes, I'm awake." I heard Christian from the bed. His voice was raspy and weak. He gave me a faint glimpse of a smile. "Come here, killer." He beckoned me over to his bedside.

"Hey bud." I said as I sat down next to his bed. "How ya feeling?"

"I've been through worse." He always would say that just so that I wouldn't worry so much, as if it ever worked.

"You look like shit." I gave him a playful smile.

"Look who's talking." He coughed and struggled to sit up.

I propped a pillow up behind him to assist in his movements. I looked down at myself and then back at him. "Yeah, well I was just a little upset."

Christian looked at me, his face went serious. "So, anything new to tell me?"

My smiled shared my face with disbelief. "How'd you know already?"

A smile, not his regular happy-go-lucky smile, but a smile, nonetheless, spread across his face. "Please. Do you honestly think he'd discuss it with your dad and not me? I think sometimes you forget he's my best friend and you're my sister." He said as he raised his eyebrows at me. "He asked me for my blessing two weeks ago. It's about time that knucklehead asked you." He paused and he dropped his smile ever so slightly. "Are you happy?"

"I've never been happier, Christian."

"Good. Marry him. Soon. Like this weekend soon." Christian laid his head back on the pillow I had placed behind him.

"Why so soon?! You plan on dying on me?" I could feel my face shift from a smile to worry.

"Nah, I don't plan on going anywhere. But life is short, why wait?" The look in his eyes was strange on the face of my best friend.

"You're right. I love him. Why wait?" I agreed. "As long as Ryker is down for it, of course I'd marry him this weekend."

"Give me a break, he would've married you months ago." There was a strain in his voice, and he let out a sigh that sounded almost relieved that I had actually agreed.

I patted his hand. "You get some rest. Ryker is going to need his best man." I walked from the lab as the reality of Ryker's question set in.

The next few days flew by. My dad hired the best wedding planner in the state, phone calls were made to the guests we wanted present who didn't already live at the compound. Ryker covered taking care of the rings. Nova, Chloe, and I found our dresses at the same upscale dress store we had gone to for my birthday. My dress was stunning. It was a light ivory, with a gentle sweetheart neckline on the completely crystal embellished bodice. The back laced up with a beautiful satin ribbon and it had a full ball gown skirt. The train had crystal embellishments around the outer edge. I opted out of the traditional heels. Instead, I chose white high-top Converse. Chloe and Nova's dresses were simple and black. They were sleeveless with a V neckline. As I tried on the dress for the last time before my wedding to Ryker, I teared up. I had never expected to be here when I first came to live at the compound. I had more now than I could ever have imagined.

Christian had developed a cough while recovering from his wounds. He refused to allow anyone to be concerned about him. He wanted everything concentrated on me and Ryker and wouldn't be told otherwise.

"You're a stubborn man. Has anyone ever told you that?" I handed him a glass of water after a fit of coughing.

"It's part of my charm." He used my own words against me and gave me a weak smile.

"That's not fair, Christian." My words came out with a touch of annoyance and a heaping helping of sadness.

"I'll be fine. Seriously. So, how're the plans coming for the big day?" He was good at changing the subject.

I gave him a serious look, but I knew it was futile to try to argue with him. "You're such a girl sometimes." I laughed as the words left my mouth. "Seeing as it's tomorrow...I hope they've all come together. You know Nova and Chloe tried to convince me into a bachelorette party?"

"Awe man, no party? That means no bachelor party!" He whined.

"Yeah, because you're in great condition to have strippers bouncing their boobs in your face." We both laughed and he began to cough again.

I handed him the glass of water again. "Seriously, dude you have got to get this checked."

"I'll be fine. Go get ready for tomorrow." He nodded to the door.

Defeated and annoyed, I started to leave and get everything finalized. Nova began to walk in as I walked out.

"Talk to him. The cough is getting worse." My voice was a hushed whisper. I looked back at him and then to her before I walked out.

Chloe and Nova insisted on keeping at least something traditional and forced me into a slumber party with them the night before my wedding. The morning of the festivities, Chloe woke me early.

There was a note and a rose on the table next to me, accompanied by a hot cup of coffee. I held the rose to my face and breathed in its floral fragrance as it softly brushed against my lips. I flipped open the note.

Good morning Doll,

Before we do this, I wanted you to know how much I love you. You've made me a better man. You have tested me and pushed ALL my buttons more than once. You're stubborn and a complete pain in the ass. But you know what you want. And the fact that you want me, makes me the happiest man in the world. I love you more than you'll ever know. I can't wait to marry you. See you in a few hours.

Love,

Your soldier boy.

His note left me on the verge of tears but for once they were happy.

"That man really IS something else." I said out loud to myself. I smiled and closed my eyes as I sniffed the rose one more time.

"Okay little missus! Time to get reeeeeeaaaaaddddddyyyyy!" Chloe sang.

"You're ridiculous." I laughed.

"Oh, hush and put this on!" She shoved a white silk robe with the word *Bride* bedazzled across the back, into my hands.

"Seriously?!" I looked at her with a face that was essentially saying, "Not a chance in hell was I putting that on."

"Oh yeah, she's serious." Nova walked out from the bathroom wearing a black silk robe with the word *Bridesmaid* bedazzled on the back. "We have hair and makeup waiting for you."

"Oh shit! She got you too?!" I cackled.

"It's okay. I had hers made especially for her." She said with a sly smile.

"Yeah. Hilarious." Chloe said with her eyes slightly squinted, as she donned a black silk robe with the words *Maid of Horror* in sparkling rhinestones on the back.

I snorted at the sight of the words. "BAHAHAHAHAHAHAHAHAHAHAHAHAHAHAHA!!!!!" I laughed, sounding a lot like Atticus.

After hours of my head being yanked on and my face being prodded, it was time to get the dress on and make my way to the "party room" as my father called it. The butterflies in my stomach began to kick up and my breathing quickened.

"Calm down, Karah. It's okay to be nervous." Nova reassured me.

"Just don't trip!" Chloe piped in with a giant smile plastered to her face.

Nova gave Chloe a look telling her to shut the hell up. They left me standing around the corner from the doors of the room to keep Ryker from seeing me before I walked down the aisle to him. The doors opened and the music began, they proceeded down. It was my turn next. I took a deep breath and shook my hands as I tried to shake away the nerves.

"Wow." My dad walked up behind me. "You look so beautiful, kiddo. You ready to do this?" He leaned in and kissed my cheek. He was dressed in one of the nicest tuxes I had ever seen, a red rose boutonniere was pinned to his tux jacket. The bruises he received from being held hostage were a deep purple and green but fading.

"Yeah, Dad, I'm ready." I took a deep breath trying to calm myself down. The butterflies in my stomach were going nuts.

"Alright then, let's do this." He held his arm out for me to take. I think for moment, he knew if he hadn't, I definitely would've tripped.

Once again, the large French doors opened. I had never seen the room as beautiful as it was now. Ivory and white satin hung from the walls tied in the center with a neat champagne colored bow. Lit candles covered the room on every available surface. Where the disco ball once hung, a dimly lit great crystal chandelier took its place. On the furthest side of the room, a dance floor, bar, tables, and chairs had been set up. Satin and roses covered the tables. Out of each center piece, a pewter candelabra was lit.

I walked towards Ryker. His crystal blue eyes reminded me of the first time I saw him as they reflected the soft lights. In a line stood Ryker, Christian in a wheelchair by his side, and Tanner was at the end. Christian and Tanner's tuxes matched my fathers. Ryker was dressed in an all-black tux. The shirt, vest, tie, and pants were all black. The head of a single red rose was pinned to his black jacket. When we reached him, my father kissed me on the cheek and handed me off to Ryker. When it was time to exchange rings, Christian handed Ryker a beautiful ring. More beautiful than I could have imagined. It was white gold with the Tree of Life at the center of two triquetras.

"You're my roots, my growth, and my forever. I love you." He smiled as he slid the ring up my finger.

The officiant, who somehow turned out to be Atticus, skipped right over the part of objections just in case Adriel decided to make an ass of himself once again. Finally, he said the words we had both been waiting to hear.

"You may now kiss the bride." The words hadn't finished leaving Atticus's mouth before Ryker grabbed me and dipped me. He smiled as he kissed me for the first time as my husband. As he lifted me back up to standing, I raised my fist high in the air like Judd Nelson at the end of The Breakfast Club.

The ceremony was flawless, and we all moved to the other side of the immense room for the reception. For the first time since I had moved to the compound a party went off without some sort of dramatic event occurring. Clay and Vanessa even came from Wyoming to celebrate our nuptials with us. I had barely recognized Vanessa. Her hair was cut into a short bob. The life returned to her eyes which had a new-found twinkle in them.

"You look so pretty, Kar!" She ran up and gave me a tight hug.

"Me?! Look at you! And you talk!" Clay, Vanessa, and I all laughed as Clay gave me a hug.

Christian wheeled his way up to us through the guests.

"Hey, speed racer!" I joked.

"Hey, MRS. Ryker!" For the first time since he was shot, he had his spark in his eyes that I had grown so used to seeing.

"Oh man, that's gonna take some getting used to." I chuckled and looked at the ring Ryker had placed on my finger.

Christian stood from his wheelchair and gave me a hug and a kiss on the forehead. "You look stunning, little sister." He said as he took both of my hands. "I'm so happy for you guys. I love you."

He began to cough again. He pulled the tissue he kept in his pocket for moments such as this, he covered his coughs with it, and as he pulled it away from his face, I could see the red splotches covering the white cloth.

"Christian?" I watched as the sparkle, that made Christian so uniquely Christian, once again disappear from his eyes and he collapsed. "CHRISTIAN!"

It had been two hours since Christian had collapsed. He had been rushed to the make-shift operating room that was still in place in the lab. My father sent the guests home as the residents of the compound waited outside the lab for the doctor to come out. After what felt like an eternity, the doctor came out. His face was solemn, and we all rushed to find out the news.

"In his initial surgery, we patched a hole the bullet caused. The repair failed and the stitches tore."

"What are you saying, Doc?" I asked, while I knew a little bit about the medical field, my brain refused to fully comprehend what the surgeon was telling us.

"His lung collapsed. The tearing from the stitches caused severe bleeding. Since he was on blood thinners to keep it from clotting around the stitches, his lung filled with blood almost instantly. I'm so sorry but Christian didn't make it."

Nova screamed, crying, she hit her knees in the middle of the hall. Atticus picked her up and sat with her in his lap on the floor. The only sound throughout the compound was the sound of Nova's cries. I could feel Ryker's hand on my shoulder as my body went numb.

∞Twelve∞

It was a quiet five days in the compound as my father arranged for Christian's service. The numbness turned into pain. The pain turned to sickness. Nova refused to eat, and I refused to leave her side. The man she loved; my brother, was gone. Ryker and Chloe traded out shifts taking care of us while Nova and I stayed in Christian's room. His clothes were still thrown in the desk chair like he would be back any minute to put them away. His meticulous use of Post-it notes stayed stuck to the sides of his computer. Chloe almost got hurt when she tried to take his pillowcases off and replace them. Nova screamed and threw the bedside lamp at her, which only made her cry harder. I tried to be the rock for her that Christian had been for me so many times before, but it was hard to do through my own grief.

The day of the funeral arrived. Atticus and Ryker helped us into the back of the black town cars parked behind the black hearse. I hadn't even noticed the cars had begun to move. After a short time, the cars lurched to a stop. As I looked out of the window, I saw rows of headstones. Under a large oak tree, chairs had been placed in neat rows next to the deep rectangular hole. I took a deep breath as Ryker opened the door, got out, and offered me his hand. His scarred hand that had a white gold band on his ring finger. I had almost forgotten I was

194

married. My heart broke more thinking of how Nova felt, the man she loved was gone. I couldn't bear to lose Ryker. After they escorted Nova, Chloe, and me to the seats set out for us, the guys returned to the hearse to carry Christian's casket. Part of me died as I watched Ryker, Atticus, Desmond, Tanner, Adriel, and my father carry the body of my brother. The tears began to fall harder and any sort of wall I had built up crumbled into a million pieces as I held onto Nova, while Christian was lowered into the ground. We each took turns dropping a rose and a handful of dirt onto the top of the casket.

The service had concluded, and we walked back to the cars, each of us were either being held or was holding someone else. I looked up the hill of the cemetery. A woman dressed in black stood on top of the hill and watched us from afar. I couldn't make out her face, but I knew she was watching, I pushed the mysterious woman from my mind. When we arrived back to the compound, my father pulled me aside, away from everyone as we walked down the hall where his office, bedroom, and lab were.

"There's something I need to give you. From Christian." His eyes glistened from the tears he refused to let me see.

My heart stopped. "What do you mean?"

"He wrote this before your wedding and told me if anything happened, to give it to you after he was buried." He extended his hand, in it was a letter.

My eyes flicked from the letter to my father and back to the paper.

My hands shook as I took it and opened it. I heard his voice as I read the last words he ever wrote me.

Hey little sister.

> *If you're reading this, I'm gone. Sorry about that. I knew there was a possibility it would happen. I made the doctor promise not to tell you there was a chance the patch may not hold. Sorry for that, too. I had to make sure you got the wedding you deserved. I know if I had said something, anything, you would have postponed your dreams. I had to make sure you went through with it. I need you to do some things for me since I'm no longer there. Watch out for Nova. Move her into my room. She'll rip the head off anyone who tries to change anything or move anything out of there. Make sure she finds love. She deserves to be happy. Obviously, no one will ever be good enough for her. Hell, I wasn't even good enough for her. But for some reason she picked me. Don't be too harsh on the next guy. Don't shut down, Ryker and Nova are going to need you as much as you need them. Make sure your dad knows how much I appreciate him and how much you appreciate him. Give Tanner my Stan Lee*

*autographed Spiderman comic. It's in your
dad's safe. Along with a ring for Nova. I want
her to have it. Make sure to tell Ryker how
much you love him every day. He's one of the
good ones. And make sure you guys have
babies. I would've made an awesome uncle. I
love you, little sister. You've been one of the
best parts of my life.*

*Love,
Christian*

P.S.- watch your language.

Any part of my heart that hadn't been
broken, shattered into dust as I finished his letter.
Tears dropped onto the page as it shook in my
hands. My back hit the wall and I slid to the floor as I
buried my face in my arms. I heard footsteps
approach and without a word, I was picked up like I
was a child off the floor. I looked up and saw who
was carrying me and it was not who I had expected.
It was Adriel. Without a word, he walked down the
hallway towards the common room where Ryker was
waiting, he passed me over to Ryker who gave him
an appreciative nod. Ryker carried me to our room
and laid me on the bed where he took my shoes off
and covered me with the blanket. All the while I
clutched the letter to my chest.

"Shhhhh. I know it's hard, but it'll get better."
I could hear a quiver in his voice. Silently, I handed
him the letter. Moments later I could hear drops as

they landed on the page and Ryker sniffled. He laid down behind me and held me as I cried myself to sleep.

It was another two days before I could muster the strength to fulfill some of the requests in Christian's letter. I got Nova moved into his room. And got the items from the safe in my dad's office. I think the ring broke Nova more than helped her. Inside the band of the solitary diamond ring, the words, *I've always loved you*, were inscribed. My stomach clenched. I gave Tanner the comic book. It was the first time I had ever seen him shed a tear. Which made Chloe cry like a chain reaction making my stomach feel sick rather than a knot.

"Babe, are you okay? You look a little green around the gills." Ryker asked as I took a step back from Tanner and Chloe.

"I'm just not feeling too hot." As the words came out, I made direct beeline to the bathroom. I spent the next thirty minutes throwing up. After brushing my teeth, I went to the bedroom and laid back on the bed.

"I called the doc. He'll be here as soon as he can, tomorrow. Can I get you anything?"

I nodded my head. "Just some water should do it."

"Coming right up, doll."

After Ryker brought me the water and a wet washcloth, I started to feel a little better.

"It's probably just a bug. Des was sick a few days ago. He spent two days hugging the toilet." I knew he was trying to be comforting but the thought of throwing up was making me nauseous again.

"Oh, sweet fuck, stop talking." I gagged and covered my mouth with both hands.

"Sorry babe." Ryker put his hand on my forehead in his sweet attempt to see if I had a fever. "When's the last time you ate something? And I mean something substantial?"

"Oh, uhm, I- I don't actually remember." Food hadn't really been a priority to me.

"Jesus Christ, woman. You're a pain in my ass." He commented with a smirk.

"Hey, you married me." I smiled a sickly smile.

"Damn right I did." His smile became wide and proud and he gave me a quick kiss. "I'm going to go get you something to eat. Please try not to throw it up."

"I make no promises." I said as I put the wet cloth over my face.

"In sickness and in health, baby." He laughed as he walked out.

Shortly after Ryker walked out, I heard a light knock on the doorframe.

"Yup?" I responded from under the cloth.

"You okay?" It was Adriel who had spoken from the doorway.

I gave him a thumbs up. "Although I might throw up again."

There was slight pause. "Ew. I'll just be going now."

"Good choice, man." Although we had been cohabitating peacefully, bugging him still brought me a certain amount of joy.

Ryker came back in. "Why'd Adriel just leave here looking paler than usual?"

I moved the cloth from my face and smiled. "He gets queasy at the thought of someone throwing up."

"You're evil and I love it." He laughed as he set down a bowl on the bedside table and took the rag from me. "Chicken and Stars."

"Thanks, soldier boy. You're the best." Slowly, I ate half the bowl and felt a little more like myself.

"You should probably get some rest. Power hurling takes a lot out of you." Ryker had sat down next to me and was rubbing his hand gently up and down my back.

I motioned to the zipper down the back of my dress, which Ryker unzipped, and I slid out of it. As I laid down, I found it easy to get comfortable. "You heard that, huh?"

"Yep." He said as he got up, tucked me under the blanket, put the wastebasket next to my side of the bed, and clicked off the lamp.

The next day, Ryker made sure I took it easy as we waited for the doctor to arrive. He propped me up on the couch. Nova finally emerged from her room. She was wearing one of Christian's favorite shirts.

I patted the seat next to me for her to come sit and join us. She sat down and laid her head on my shoulder.

"How ya feeling?" My eyes glanced over to where her head was resting on my shoulder.

"Like my heart was ripped out and my soul was destroyed. You?" Her voice was flat and sad.

"About the same. Plus add puking my brains out."

"Gross. Don't puke on me please." She said quietly. I hated hearing her sad, but at least she was able to make a joke. That's a step forward.

"Deal." I smiled slightly.

Around three pm, the doctor finally arrived. Ryker walked with me and the doctor to the lab. I hesitated before stepping foot into the room. It was where I got the worst news of my life, so I had been avoiding it altogether, since Christian died. I forced myself to go in, it had been reverted back to its state previous to Christian's surgery, with a little encouragement from Ryker. The doctor proceeded to do a standard workup.

"It seems to look like a bout of food poisoning. Have you eaten anything off lately?"

Ryker looked at me, with pleading to be honest with the doctor in his face. I complied with his request. "That would probably require me to be eating in general."

The doctor shot Ryker a concerned look as I told him the truth. "Has anyone else been sick in the compound lately?" He asked as he scribbled notes on his chart.

"Des was a few days ago." Ryker told the doctor. "Why, did he get her sick?" I knew he would give Des unnecessary heckling for getting me sick.

"It's probably just be a stomach bug. I wouldn't worry too much. I do want to put you on an IV to make sure you're staying hydrated while we wait on these test results. I want to make sure there's no sort of side effects from the experiments you endured as a child."

"Can she have the IV anywhere else than here? I can take her anywhere else, just not here." Ryker asked the doctor. His tone was firm but not aggressive.

"Uhm. Yeah, sure. That should be okay." The doctor had confusion in his voice as to why we wouldn't want to be in the lab, but thankfully, he didn't press the matter.

The doctor stuck the needle into the back of my hand, taped it down, and hung the fluids on a rolling IV pole.

"Thank you." I mouthed to Ryker. I had the overwhelming feeling he didn't want to be there any more than I did.

"You're welcome." He whispered as he kissed the top of my head.

Ryker brought me back to our room. As I laid on the bed with my back propped against the headboard, he grabbed his jacket. "I have to go for a little while, I'll be back in a bit."

"Yeah, sure. Where are you going?"

"Nowhere to worry about. I just need to go talk to Christian." He had gone almost every day since Christian was buried to s t and talk to his grave.

"You're going to his grave?" I hadn't been yet, but I knew I needed to go soon.

"Yeah, they're delivering his headstone today." He replied as he slid his arms into the leather sleeves and pulled it up across his shoulders.

"Okay baby. I love you."

"I love you, too. Please stay in bed. If you absolutely HAVE to get up, get Chloe to help you. PLEASE." He begged.

With a smirk, I appeased his mind. "Yes sir."

An hour went by before there was a knock on the door.

"Come in." I replied to the knock.

The doctor hesitantly entered the room.

"Oh, hey, Doc. Ready to take this needle out of me?"

"Yes, but first…" He held up a piece of paper. "I got your test results back." He handed the page to me.

As I read it, my eyes widened. "Oh, fuck." I whispered.

The doctor removed the IV and put a small bandage over the hole the needle left. "Do you have any questions?"

"Nope," I said quietly, as I continued to process what the test results said.

I had been waiting on the couch with Chloe, Nova, and Tanner when Ryker returned with Atticus and Des. Shortly after, Adriel walked in from the hall, cautiously.

"Are you contagious?" Adriel asked as he kept as far away from me as he possibly could.

"Not exactly." My eyes squinted slightly.

"Not exactly?" Ryker asked confused. "What's going on babe?"

"I'm not contagious but I DO have a bug." I remarked as Ryker took off his jacket and flung it on the back of the couch.

"Then how are you not contagious?!" Adriel asked backing up a few steps.

"Thanks Des." Ryker addressed Des sarcastically.

"Me?!" Des exclaimed. "I wasn't contagious. But I did learn we have to clean out the fridge more. I got food poisoning from some old chili." He visibly shivered.

Ryker's confusion etched deeper on his face.

"No, babe. Des didn't get me sick. YOU did." I paused for a moment to see if he'd catch on which he clearly didn't. "I'm pregnant!" I laughed.

"Yeah, that definitely wasn't me." Des began to laugh as well.

Ryker ran to where I was sitting and leaned over me with a hand next to me on the couch. "Pregnant?! You're sure?!" I had never seen such a big smile on his face before as he put his free hand on my stomach.

"Yeah, I'm sure. The doctor told me after you left." I returned his smile with my own.

"Oh goodie. A screaming, crying, puking baby Ryker." Adriel said grumpily.

"Well, actually, according to this..." I held up the paper the doctor had given me. "Its TWO screaming, crying, puking baby Rykers."

∞Thirteen∞

"Twins?!" Ryker exclaimed as he dropped to his knees in front of where I sat on the couch, to gain a closer proximity to my stomach housing his two children.

At the moment of Ryker's exclamation, my father, Uncle Reed, and Marcus entered the common area from my father's office. Dad's face phased to confusion as he walked in on the scene. "What's, uh, what's happening here?" He pointed to Ryker on his knees, holding me.

I locked eyes with my dad. "Hey there, Grandpa." My smile grew wider across my face.

"Grandpa? I'm not that old." It took my father a moment to connect the dots and his face lit up. "Oh! GRANDPA?!" He hugged me and turned to Ryker, shaking his hand, and sat down next to me, opposite Nova. "Wait...you guys JUST got married...how are you already- "He cut off his own thought before finishing it. "Ya know what, never mind." He put both hands up in front of him to stop any comments on the subject before they began.

Ryker and I exchanged a knowing glance as my father started talking to my stomach. "Hey, there little one this is your Pops."

"Uhm, Thomas..." Ryker paused as he waited for my father to look at him.

"What? Can't you see I'm in the middle of a conversation here?" He pointed to my stomach.

"Yeah, but you may want to broaden the conversation...since there's two in there." Ryker held up two fingers and laughed as the shock took over my father's face.

"Twins?! Oh, dear lord, help us." My father laughed a deep laugh.

Chloe had become irritatingly excited and was bouncing in place, her fists next to her face were vibrating. "That means we get to throw a baby shower!"

"Calm down there, Spaky. You really think a party is a good idea?" I asked. I didn't want to step foot into the party room. It still hurt far too much to even think about the events that took place the last time I had been in there.

"Of course!" She read my mind as she continued. "We'll do it here, in the common area. Just the people you want, no extra guests." She knew there was no way Nova and I would step foot into the party room, regardless of the extravagance that laid behind the doors.

I rolled my eyes at the thought of another event taking place, but I knew it would be better to appease her than to fight her on it.

"I'll help her plan everything. I need something to distract me." Nova added from her seat next to me. It made me feel better about the entire thing knowing she was wanting to help, especially after what Christian had said about being an uncle.

"I'll prepare the food!" Atticus had bellowed from across the room. He had recently developed a love for cooking. Unfortunately, he made meals large enough for a compound full of people his size.

"NO!" Chloe, Nova, and I exclaimed in chorus.

"Atti, I love you man, but I'm already going to get huge, I don't need to add literal feasts to that weight gain." I laughed. Atticus's face dropped into a child-like pout as Chloe crossed the room to him.

"It's okay big guy" She gave his arm a placating pat. "You can help Nova and I taste test the caterers." Instantly, Atticus's face brightened back up.

Adriel lifted from the wall he had been leant against and walked a few steps towards us. I mild look of defeat was across his face. "Congratulations. But don't expect me to babysit or even touch them."

Ryker's eyes narrowed and I looked at Adriel with my eyebrows raised. "Yeah, about that, don't worry. I would NEVER ask you to." I told him.

I had all but forgotten Marcus and Uncle Reed had entered the room with my father until Marcus spoke.

"You realize, you won't be able to train, right?" He paused. "We have no idea what kind of effect your powers will have on the fetuses." His hands were in their usual place behind his back.

"He's right." Uncle Reed added. "For all we know, they could have powers of their own since

Ryker and you both do. I would also recommend you don't attempt a natural birth. The stress on your body from labor could attack the babies."

At his words, Ryker took my hand. His face went from joy to worry and I could tell the wheels in his head were turning. I gave his hand a gentle, reassuring squeeze.

After everyone's fawning and congratulations, Ryker and I decided it was time for us to take a moment for ourselves and went to our bedroom. It was a bit of a sensory overload with everyone talking at once.

Ryker closed the door and rested his forehead on it. "Reed is right, Karah." He turned to me, keeping his eyes focused on the floor. "We have no idea what this kind of thing can do to your powers."

I grabbed both of his hands in mine and gently led him to the bed. His skin had gone pale and he still refused to make eye contact. "Hey. Look at me." I craned my face down to his and he raised his eyes. "We're going to be fine. All four of us will make it through this just fine."

"How can you be sure? We aren't like everyone else." His voice was full of fear and worry. I could tell he was more stressed than I had ever seen him before.

"THAT'S how I'm sure. It's because we aren't like everyone else that I know we can do this and be okay." Christian's words filled my head. "Plus..." I paused for a moment. "We've been through worse." He gave my hands a gentle squeeze and smiled at the words.

"I love you, doll."

"I love you too, soldier boy." I leaned in and gave him a gentle kiss.

It had been six months since the announcement of our pregnancy. As my belly grew, my irritability also expanded with my waistline. Which was partially due to the new flow of hormones rushing through me and mostly because of the two children using my bladder as a punching bag. My favorite place had seemed to become the common area couch with its immediate adjacency to the kitchen and the bathroom. Ryker waited on me hand and foot and my father had begun construction of what I could only assume was a nursery in the room I stayed in when I first came to the compound. Chloe and Nova began planning the baby shower while the rest of the team made it their focus to find Anna. They knew to never make contact if they did. They were only to do recon and report, I wanted to know where she was at every move. As soon as I was able to get back in the field, I was going to take her down myself.

I had been sitting on the couch enjoying my new and strange craving of eggrolls dipped in chocolate pudding when Adriel had entered the room. He was wearing nothing but a towel as he went to grab a drink.

"Dude, put some clothes on!" I snapped.

"I'm just getting a drink. I'll be- "He stopped as he saw the plate in front of me. "What in the world are you eating?" His face contorted into disgust.

I narrowed my eyes at him. "Get. Away. From me." I growled.

"That's truly nauseating." He pointed to the plate.

"I will end you." I glared at him.

"Hmm. Pregnancy seems to have made you cranky. Well, crankier!" He let out an annoying laugh at his own joke.

"Yup. I'm gonna stab you. Right in the chest." I nonchalantly replied to his laughter.

He laughed harder as he walked out of the common area and back toward his room. I was tempted to throw an eggroll at the back of his head but thought against it. Uncle Reed had come in from the lab as I put down what would have been a very well-aimed eggroll.

"Hey, Karah." He looked at the plate and grimaced. "After you finish with...THAT..." he motioned at the plate. "I want to do an ultrasound and check on the babies."

"Okay." My voice was muffled by the large bite I had just taken.

"So weird." He mumbled as he walked away.

As I finished my delicious pregnancy delicacy, I made my way to the bedroom to find Ryker. He hated to miss anything related to the twins. He wasn't in the room, which was odd, since that's normally where he was if he wasn't with me. As I pulled my phone from my back pocket, I could hear his voice coming from the hall leading to the front door. I slowly but surely made my way to meet him.

"Hey baby." He gave me a quick kiss on the cheek and rubbed my belly.

"Where were you?" My face was clearly more confusion than anything else. He rarely left the compound without letting me know he was going somewhere.

"I went to see Christian." Ryker and I made it a point to go once a week to replace the flowers and sit under the oak tree.

"Oh." I sounded slightly disappointed that he went without me.

"I just needed to talk to him, nothing to worry about."

"Why didn't you tell me you were leaving?" I asked him, the irritability was clear in my voice.

"Well, you were eating, and I know better than to disrupt THAT process." He laughed.

My tone softened. "Fa r point." I smiled and rolled my eyes. "You got back just in time. Uncle Reed wants to do an ultrasound."

"Oh good!" He always got excited when we got to see the babies. "So, what were the Beans craving this time, by the way?" he asked as he walked, and I waddled, toward the lab.

"Eggrolls and chocolate pudding."

He turned to look at me. "Gross." He chuckled.

My father had purchased an ultrasound machine the day after I told him about the twins. He was adamant about Ryker and being able to check on them whenever we wanted. Which worked out seeing as we wanted to see them often. Reed rolled the machine over to the table I had immediately laid on.

"Comfortable?" he asked before squeezing the cold jelly on my expanded abdomen.

"Not for the past six months." I replied with a laugh.

As he pressed the wand to my stomach, the screen filled with the familiar black and white. The shapes of their little faces were clear.

He moved the wand to the other side. "Want to know their sexes?"

I looked at Ryker with a beaming smile. "Of course, I do!" I dropped my smile slightly. "Because, you know, Chloe is going to want to know for the shower." Ryker gave me a wink and smiled the smile I loved so much.

"Alright. Baby A," He pointed to the screen and I took a deep breath in. "is a little boy. And baby B." he moved his hand across to the other baby. "Right there, kicking their brother in the butt, is a little girl."

I let the breath I was holding, out. "A boy AND a girl." I looked up at Ryker. He had never looked so proud. "Let's hope they're more like you than they are me."

Uncle Reed took measurements of both the babies before wiping the jelly from my stomach and him and Ryker helped me sit up. I felt like a turtle who had fallen on their back.

"Guess I should go find Chloe." I said as I attempted to hop off the table.

"Okay baby, you go ahead, I want to talk to Reed about a couple things really quick."

"Oh...uhm...okay." I didn't know what he would need to talk to Uncle Reed about but I'm sure it had something to do with our delivery options.

I toddled from the lab and up the hall toward the common area to find Chloe. She met me as she sprinted across the room and began jumping up and down.

"A BOY AND A GIIIIIIRRRRRL!" she squealed.

"Eavesdropper." I laughed.

Two months later, it was finally time for the baby shower that Chloe and Nova had been planning. That morning, I began to have pain that radiated through my back. The pain had happened before, which Uncle Reed immediately had a colleague, who was an obstetrician, come in and check. It turned out to be Braxton-Hicks contractions, but it still hurt like hell.

"You okay, Karah?" Ryker asked as he saw me rub my back and sides of my now enormous belly.

"Yeah, just a little sore. Don't worry." I knew telling him not to worry was pointless, because he constantly worried, the closer it came to the time of the twin's arrival. We had decided on a scheduled cesarean section to make sure my body didn't go on the defensive and hurt the babies.

"You ready for today?" He stretched as he rolled out of bed.

I laid back across the bed and looked at him upside-down. "We both know this shower isn't about me. Everyone just wants to spoil the babies and they aren't even here yet." I laughed.

"Yeah, that's probably true." He replied with a shrug and a smile of his own.

I attempted to sit up with a great deal of struggling. Ryker walked around to the side of the bed and looked down at me. "You're stuck, aren't you?" He began laughing loudly.

I stared at the ceiling before replying. "Yeah. Yeah, I am." I joined in his laughter and he grabbed both of my hands, hoisting me up.

After we both got ready for the day, we made our way to the kitchen. While I couldn't drink the coffee I wanted, Ryker agreed to let me have decaf, which did not help my morning grumpiness. As we walked into the common area, pink and blue balloons and decorations covered the entire room. Three tables had been set up against the large glass windows, covered with pink and blue tablecloths and tiny little pacifiers. The kitchen island has been covered with the same tablecloths and the skeleton of what appeared to be a buffet line had been put up.

"Whoa. That is a LOT of colors." My eyes grew wide as I tried to absorb all the hues in the room.

"Well, to be fair it IS Chloe." Ryker shrugged.

Chloe had come bounding in the room. "Okay, so you guys are gonna have to leave for like an hour. Okie dokie?!" Her voice was downright giddy.

"Yes ma'am." I told her. I could see how happy she was putting this all together.

Ryker and I decided to go visit Christian. I had to talk to him even if he wasn't there to talk back. As we pulled up to his grave, I looked to Ryker.

"Can you give me a minute. I kind of want to talk to him alone for a little bit."

"Sure thing, doll. Do you need help getting out of the car?"

I chuckled lightly. "No, I think I got it." After only a slight struggle to get out of the car, I finally made it to the bench next to Christian's plot.

I sighed as I sat down. "Hey, big brother." I paused almost as though I was expecting to hear his voice. "Would you just look at this?" I rubbed my belly that the twins were occupying. "I wish you were here for this and they could've met their Uncle Christian." As I spoke, tears silently slid from my eyes. "Chloe and Nova set up this huge baby shower. It's a little bit ridiculous but it makes them happy." I wiped the tears from my face and sniffled. "I miss you." As the words left my mouth, I saw Ryker step out of the driver's side and beckoned me with a wave of his hand. I tottered my way back to the car.

"What's up?" I was breathing heavily. It took much more effort to relocate my enormous bulk.

"Chloe called, they finished setting up early." He cocked his head as he looked at me. "You okay?"

"Yeah, I'm okay. I just miss him."

Ryker wrapped me in a hug and kissed my forehead. "I know baby. Me too."

When we entered the common area of the compound, the tables were now completely covered.

One had gifts piled high, the second had some sort of crafting accoutrement, and the third had assorted party favors. I glanced over to Ryker.

"You think there's enough stuff happening here?" I whispered with a short laugh.

Everyone had gathered in the room including Clay and Vanessa. Standing at the back of the room was a man I didn't recognize. He shared a striking resemblance to Ryker. An almost identical resemblance. His hair was cut short and his stature wasn't near as muscular. He also didn't have the scars that Ryker had but he did have the same piercing blue eyes.

"Uhm, babe." I got Ryker's attention and his eyes followed my gaze.

"Ah shit." His voice sounded annoyed.

"Ryker, who is that?" I asked. It was never a good thing when he sounded irritated.

"I forgot I told him you were having a baby shower. That would be your brother-in-law, my twin, Aiden." He walked towards his brother.

"My huh-, your what-?!" I stumbled over my own inarticulate words. "Wait! So, this is double your fault?!" I pointed with both index fingers at my belly.

"Hey brother. Couldn't have called when you got married?!" Aiden greeted Ryker.

"There's a reason I didn't call. You don't know how to behave yourself." Ryker replied dryly but with a smile. "Why are you here?"

"Are you kidding me? Like I'd miss this. I would have come to the wedding, too, by the way. So, I'm going to have a niece?" He looked around the room for a moment. "A nephew?"

"Both. Aiden, why are you really here?"

"Both?! Well, look at that. Like their old man." He completely ignored Ryker's last question and looked past Ryker to me. "So, this must be the missus!" he addressed me reaching his hand out. "You're...whoa...you're uhm, glow- "

I cut him off before he could finish his sentence as I held up one finger. "If you say glowing, I will set you on fire, right now. I am not glowing, but I am currently reaching Shamu status." I gestured around my belly.

He smiled and was slightly taken aback by my threat. He turned to face Ryker. "I like her!" he laughed.

Suddenly, I had the over whelming urge to pee...again. After leaving the bathroom, the cramping I had felt earlier that morning rushed over me again. As the aching sensation began to subside, a gush of liquid ran down the inside of my thighs, covering my pants and shoes. I stepped back and looked down at the puddle forming at my feet.

"Oh great." I whispered to myself and calmly rejoined the others.

"Uh, babe. We gotta go. Like...now." I told him lightly trying to breathe through the pain.

"What's wrong, babe?" He turned to face me as he asked. His eyes locked on my pants and quickly shifted to my eyes.

"My water just broke all over my shoes." I replied with a pout and the room went silent.

Almost as quickly as the room fell silent, voices started to chime all together at once.

"I'll get the bags!" cried Chloe as she took off running toward Ryker's and my room.

"I'll get the car!" Des had already grabbed the keys and was headed toward the door.

My dad and Ryker helped me to the car as I continued to try to breathe through the contractions.

The pain grew worse and the crashing waves of cramps came closer together as we neared the hospital. Every person in the compound convoyed behind us. Atticus and my dad ran in the emergency room doors ahead of everyone, shortly returning with a wheelchair and hospital staff. Instantly, we were taken to a delivery room.

I could hear Ryker yelling in the hall. "No! No way! It's not safe for her or the babies!"

"It's too late, we can't stop the process now. That's even riskier. Now get your ass in there and make sure her stress levels don't get too high!" Reed was trying to reason with him.

Ryker entered, followed by the doctor and multiple nurses, pushing newborn incubators.

"You ready, Karah?" The doctor asked as he sat at the foot of the bed and the nurses took the blankets off me. Ryker took the seat next to me and grabbed my hand. I could see he was scared.

Another wave of painful contractions hit. "Not particularly!" I groaned through gritted teeth. I looked at Ryker. "Just know, right now, in this moment, I HATE you."

"That's fine, baby. Just take it out on my hand." He replied with a smirk.

"Well, get ready because I can see the early bird's head. On the count of three, tuck your chin to your chest and push, okay? One...two...three, push!" The doctor encouraged me.

I pushed and felt like the bones in the lower half of my body where shattering. I stopped pushing and began panting. I could feel the beads of sweat forming on my forehead.

"Head is out, time for the shoulders!" The doctor exclaimed. "Another big push on the count of three. One...two...three, push." He repeated.

With the second round I pushed as hard as I could, releasing a pain-filled scream. Ryker wiped the sweat from my head and patted my hand that had been crushing his.

The pain was beginning to lessen as I heard the tiny cries from the foot of the bed. A nurse walked over and carefully revealed the squishy pink baby. "Say hello to your son."

No sooner as the words came from her mouth, the next excruciating wave hit.

"You're doing fantastic, baby." Ryker kissed my forehead and wiped my hair from my face.

"This is your fault!!" I snarled as the pain intensified again. "I think they're trying to rip me in half!"

Ryker's smile quickly faded. "Babe, you need to calm down okay?" His voice hushed to just below a whisper. "Your eyes, they're silver." His tone returned to normal. "Deep breaths. It's almost over."

I closed my eyes, rested my head back on the pillow, and took several deep breaths.

"Look at me, doll." Ryker said as he kissed my hand.

I obliged his request, looking into his perfect blue eyes. I could feel myself calming and the wave dissipated. Moments later, the pain began again.

"Here comes baby number two." I had almost forgotten the doctor was at the foot of the bed staring directly into my business.

Twenty minutes of pushing and searing pain later, little miss stubborn arrived to join her brother. After about an hour and a half, Ryker and I stayed alone with the babies.

"You did it, babe." His eyes never left the face of our daughter. "She looks just like you. And apparently is just as stubborn as her momma, too." A smile hadn't left his face since he laid eyes on the twins.

Finally, our family was allowed in to meet the newest members of the compound. My father instantly grabbed one baby, Nova the other. Chloe was peeking on her tip toes to see over Nova's shoulder. Adriel stayed against the wall since babies freak him out.

Aiden immediately gave Ryker a hug, clapping his hand against his brothers' back. "Congratulations, man."

"Oh, Karah, they're beautiful." Chloe said from behind Nova.

"Hey, kiddo" Dad whispered as his thumb gently stroked the tiny fist wrapped around his finger. I could see his eyes glisten in the bright lights of the hospital room.

Nova finally relinquished holding rights over to Atticus. Our daughter looked so tiny cradled in his monstrous arms. Meanwhile, Des and Reed moved in closer around Atticus to look at the baby.

Uncle Reed looked to Ryker. "How was her stress?" He nodded to me.

"Well, her eyes went silver for a minute there."

"Silver? Well, that's new." Uncle Reed furrowed his brow and scratched his chin.

"Did you guys ever decide on names?" Nova asked as she moved to see our son that my father still refused to allow anyone else to hold.

Ryker and I exchanged smiles. "Yeah. We did." I answered.

"What are we calling the tiny beans?" Tanner asked, he refused to touch either of the babies out of fear he'd hurt or drop them.

"The girl is Ashleigh Elane Ryker." I paused and took Ryker's hand as my eyes went from Nova to my father. "The boy is Christian Thomas Ryker."

Made in the USA
Columbia, SC
16 September 2024

42321621R00126